MW01632901

The Clue of the Clever Canine

The Clue of the Clever Canine

Lee Tyler

VANTAGE PRESS
New York

Although there most certainly is a Burlingame, California, there is no Park Plaza Apartments, and all of the characters depicted in this story are also drawn from the author's imagination.

FIRST EDITION

Published by Vantage Press, Inc.
516 West 34th Street, New York, New York 10001

Manufactured in the United States of America
ISBN: 0-533-10892-6

Library of Congress Catalog Card No.: 93-94962

0 9 8 7 6 5 4 3 2 1

To Geoffrey St. John Cornish, who spurred me on

Contents

The Cast

Residents of the Park Plaza Apartments (also known as the "Dog House")

1st Floor:	Laura Fiedler, manager The Chin family and Ming, a Shih-Tzu Merv Allen
2nd Floor:	Bob Delaware and Gigi, his poodle
3rd Floor:	Nancy Webb and Angus, her Scottie Elsie Johnson, victim
4th Floor:	Leon Levin George Schmidt and Hans, his dachshund
5th Floor:	Ruth Kenny and Millie, a mutt Stella Rankin
6th Floor:	Mimi Masterson Helen Emmons and Pepper, her spaniel

and

Detective Harry Winslow, Burlingame Police Department
Officer June Jacobs, BPD, and K-9 partner, the shepherd Chief
Don, the mailman
Pete Graves, locksmith

The Clue of the Clever Canine

1
June

Cruising her patrol that sunny Wednesday morning in March, June Jacobs smiled to herself. A happy and positive soul, she gloried in the beauty of the early spring day in the peaceful, pretty San Francisco suburb where she'd lived her entire twenty-seven years. She was smiling, too, at the personal pride in having come as far as she had in her three short years with the Burlingame Police Department.

Five feet six, blond, brown-eyed, and pert, she was a very shapely young woman. Even her severe mannish uniform could not disguise her feminine curves. June was not unaware of her good looks. Rather, she took them for granted and often sought to downplay them, such as now as she reached up to push a frivolous errant curl back under her no-nonsense cap.

From as far back as she could remember, June had wanted to be a policeperson. Police work ran in her family. She was the daughter of a cop, no longer living. Her aunt, a portrait artist, did eye-witness sketches for the San Mateo Police Department.

June had worked hard to make her dream job come true, and here she was with her own patrol car and a wonderful partner, the shepherd "Chief" of the K-9 Corps. She had an easy rapport with dogs.

In the rear-view mirror, she glanced, amused. Chief

was sitting up as tall as a man on the backseat behind the wire screen. Alert and grinning, with his rows and rows of sharp, gleaming white teeth, he was ready for come what may during his shift.

To certain townspeople peering into the police car, blatantly painted with the white-on-black warning POLICE DOG STAND CLEAR, Chief looked like a "killer dog." June chuckled at the thought. For nothing could be more untrue. Work to her dog was not a job, but play. During their eight hours on duty, he might be called upon to roust a burglar, corner a thief, break up a fist fight, chase a speeder. But usually his fierce appearance, big bristly body, black fur on brown, and face like a bandit's mask served in itself to squelch trouble before it began. Not that there ever was much trouble in this quiet little town where nothing dramatic ever seemed to happen. She sighed.

They'd been together since the dog was weaned from his mother. June had raised and obedience-trained Chief. And when she'd decided to enter police work, she'd hoped he would have that aptitude, too. Happily, he did, and after she had earned her badge they had gone through specialized schooling together. Chief lived at her home, slept on her bed, and when not on duty was loving and playful. One just couldn't ask for a better companion.

"How ya doin'?" She smiled at him in the mirror.

She slowed for a moment along Floribunda Avenue to admire an almond blossom tree at the height of its showiest pinkness.

Burlingame was known for its lovely floral appearance. Two years after the famous San Francisco earthquake of 1906, the town had been settled by tradesmen and servants employed by the many wealthy people moving down to safer land in the elegant adjacent community of Hillsborough. Many of these servants were gardeners, who'd left their beauty marks all about the town in the form of manicured hedges, neat lawns, lots of flowers.

A crackling voice over the intercom interrupted June's thoughts. "This is a nine-one-one, nine-one-one," the female dispatcher repeated. "Proceed to the Park Plaza Apartments. Possible homicide," the dispatcher added, an incredulous tone to her voice.

June felt a flutter of excitement at the adventure waiting. The girl in her wanted to flick the switch on the dashboard that activated the car's siren and flashing beacon. But her professional self cautioned against unduly upsetting the neighborhood. She settled for stepping on the accelerator. "Here we go, Chief!" she announced. Into her voice radio she flatly said in the approved protocol, "Car Six, responding."

"You know something?" she said to the dog as they sped through the streets. She had no compulsion about talking aloud to him; he was a lot smarter than many people she knew. "They call where we're going 'the Dog House.' You know why?"

His ears snapped to attention.

"Because they're the only apartments in this town where dogs are allowed. You may find this interesting!" She smiled at him in the mirror.

Getting the gist, Chief shifted on his haunches, staring intently ahead. . . .

2
Plaza

The big brown- and cream-colored building known as the Park Plaza Apartments dominated the corner of El Camino and Chapin. It was generally considered the best rental address in Burlingame. From the outside, it would never take a beauty prize. Ah, but inside, what a delight. Large rooms. Picture windows. Thickly padded long, wide hallways. And all so safe and secure.

Only residents with their own specially coded key could get into the Plaza. It was virtually impossible for anyone who didn't "belong" there to enter. (Unless some careless tenant allowed a stranger in without checking. But Laura Fiedler, the diligent and motherly manager, had residents pretty well trained about that.) To be a resident of the Park Plaza was like being a member of one big happy family. Maybe you didn't know everyone's last name, but you probably knew their first and certainly the face.

There were six floors to the building, connected by an agonizingly slow (if you were in a hurry) elevator. Get off at the wrong floor and you were bound to find something of interest happening, for many a resident found the hallway ideal for recreational purposes.

On the second floor, Bob Delaware, a golf fanatic and one of the six dog owners in the building, liked to practice long putts.

Lola, a ballroom dancing teacher on 5, found her hallway ideal for practicing new steps. By herself, without partner or music.

Arnold, one of the many elderly tenants, who lived on 4, prided himself on keeping fit by marching from one end of his hall to the other. It reminded him, he'd explain to anyone who'd listen, of the promenades he'd taken on cruise ships in his youth. Ten times 'round the deck equaled a mile.

Nancy Webb, a working girl and occupant of Apartment 302, also made good use of her hallway. Every night, when she got home from work, she let her Scottie, Angus, run free in it. To atone for leaving him alone all day, she had taught the dog what she thought was a harmless game—to fetch and retrieve Elsie Johnson's evening newspaper at 308, at the far end of the hall.

Elsie, a stately but gregarious white-haired widow, had long ago agreed to the game for she, too, had a playful streak. Smilingly watching through her peephole at game time, Elsie would throw open the door as the dog returned her paper and cry out with praise, "Thanks, Angus!"

The bright-eyed dog did not play this daily game just for the sport of it. Elsie always rewarded him with a couple of crunchy Milkbones. Sometimes Elsie would tease him, making him beg, which would prompt him to bark, a definite sin at the Plaza. But eventually he would collect, gobble the biscuits greedily, grin his thanks, and race home to his own apartment, which Nancy casually left ajar. So went the routine on an early Monday evening in March.

The game was over. The dog had reentered 302 now, and stood before Nancy, saucily planted on his sturdy short legs, and panting. He was exceedingly pleased with himself. "Good boy!" Nancy said, affectionately patting his soft, fuzzy head.

She got up and walked to the door to close it. As she did so, she waved down the hall toward 308 with a friendly gesture of greeting. But Elsie never saw it.

3
The Hostess

Immediately upon giving Angus his biscuit, and an extra one for the begging she had made him do, Elsie retreated inside her apartment. She was expecting a guest in for cocktails shortly and was anxious to do some extra primping for this friend was one of her favorite people.

About an hour later, Elsie was satisfied with her appearance. And right on time she heard her bell. Swiftly, she moved to the door. She gave one final glance in the hall mirror and approvingly fluffed her pretty white hair.

Despite her advanced years, a number she chose to keep secret, she was a picture-perfect image of a with-it senior citizen. This early evening she was dressed in her favorite outfit—expensive, blousy sweater, well-cut slacks that trimmed her derriere, and spike-heeled pumps—all in white that set off her hair. Her makeup was just-so, producing a healthy, tawny glow. Her cheeks, discreetly blushed.

With a much-practiced smile, she opened the door. "Hello!" she chirruped, standing on tiptoe and offering her face for the expected kiss. "Come in!"

Her eyes swept him from head to toe, approvingly until she noticed his footwear. Really, the man could be so Bohemian sometimes! Tennis shoes when invited for cocktails! Chidingly, she said, "Having a problem with your feet, dear?"

He grinned that delightful crooked way he had that always won her over, and she decided not to say any more about it. She was, after all, awfully glad to have him visit.

Leading her guest to her cheerful, cluttered living room, she waved to a choice of seats. There was a fancifully carved, straight-backed hardwood she'd borrowed from the dining area, a soft squashy chair, and a chintz-covered sofa. The guest chose the squashy chair.

"Now, you just make yourself comfortable, dear," Elsie said. "I'll go mix the drinks." Happily humming, she headed for the kitchen.

For twenty years, Elsie had lived alone, and she always looked forward to entertaining. Few cronies of her own age were still living. No matter. She really preferred younger people anyway, and there were plenty to choose from in such a large place as the Plaza.

She often invited her neighbors in, preferably one at a time, "so I can get to know you better." Her invitations were always at her favorite time of day, the cocktail hour. And they were eagerly accepted, for it was a badge of distinction to be singled out by Elsie. As the oldest "grande dame" at the Park Plaza Apartments, and the wealthiest resident besides (she made no secret of that), Elsie had clout.

Not everybody liked her. Her sometimes haughty, imperious ways put some people off. Certain of her affectations made others cringe. She liked to call her guests "dear" or "darling," even if she'd just met them yesterday. And she had an inhospitable quirk: she insisted that her guests stay out of her way and not talk while she was preparing the refreshments. "My kitchen is too small for two people," she'd explain. "And I can't hear what you're saying when I'm in here and you're out there."

Neither was true. Her hearing was fine. Her kitchen wasn't too small at all. Fact of the matter is, she relished the prelude to hostessing. She loved to prolong the moments before encounter by dawdling; slowly doling the ice cubes, painstakingly measuring the jiggers with the liquor, spreading cheese on the crackers with infinite care. Guests who'd been to Elsie's more than once knew the routine: they were expected to sit, stay put, and wait patiently.

Elsie disliked anyone roaming around her living room. She had many interesting and expensive things on display—paintings, rare books, art objects. They were on the walls, on the tables, and in a handsome glass-doored corner cabinet. Guests were expected to notice and admire them. But from a distance; never to touch.

Even her umbrella stand held extraordinary objects. Along with a genuine London bumbershoot were several tall stiff sticks of obvious value: a fireplace poker dating to Colonial days, a branding iron from the heyday of the American West, and several antique golf clubs.

On her coffee table, she always kept the latest best seller and an eclectic collection of magazines. The stack usually included *Bon Appetit, Lear's, Connoisseur, Time*. Maybe even a sports magazine, for Elsie prided herself on being up-to-date on many subjects.

Place of honor, traditionally, was given to the latest *New Yorker*. Her guest would likely have scanned the whole issue, checked every cartoon, and stifled a chuckle or two by the time Elsie finally emerged with the drinks. (Never would a guest laugh out loud, unless Elsie was in the same room to appreciate the joke. That was another of her house rules.)

Usually, the first drink was a long time coming. But not this particular night. In much less time than usual, Elsie emerged from the kitchen. Her guest was caught red-handed. Elsie's merry mood instantly vanished.

"Really!" she huffed. "What nerve!"

Her guest reacted calmly. Elsie indignantly raised her voice. The guest spoke louder, too. Finally, Elsie's voice became insistent and shrill. So did that of her guest. Incendiary words were exchanged.

Suddenly, an icy calm settled over Elsie. She turned and placed the drinks she had so meticulously prepared on the dining table. She wheeled about again, facing her guest, and stood defiantly in the middle of her living room.

Only five feet two, even in her spike heels, she puffed up in anger like a ruffled grouse. Arms folded, shoulders back, chest out, Elsie demanded that her guest leave. Right now.

It happened so fast she never had time to scream. The last she knew, a low, guttural, animallike sound erupted from her guest—this charming, witty guest she always looked forward to seeing.

Strong hands seized her around the throat and squeezed tighter... tighter. She gasped for air, making gagging noises. Suddenly, she was released, with a violent shove.

Shocked with pain and surprise, she lost her balance. One of her spike heels snapped, and she fell backwards against the dining table, striking her head sharply against an ornately carved hardwood chair, twin to the one in the living room. She slid to the floor. In a matter of moments she was dead.

Small and still, she lay, mouth agape, her life's blood scarcely visible on the outside but, inside her head, fatally drowning her brain. Her eyes stared in fixed astonishment at this unexpected turn of events.

Her visitor stepped around her body, hastened towards the door, opened it, checked the hallway to be sure that no one was there. And fled.

4
Meanwhile

Sneakily, the killer let himself into his own apartment. Breathing hard, he kicked off his shoes and hurled them into the farthest recess of his bedroom closet. He'd noticed, leaving Elsie's, that a trailing shoelace had picked up a trace of her blood. Just a trace. It had surprised him how little her head wound had bled.

He remembered stooping close to her to make sure she was dead. That must have been how the blood got on his shoe. Damn. Well, he would wash it off later. Right now what he needed was a drink to calm his nerves. He gulped one down with such haste that he coughed, but the rush of warmth that the liquor accomplished made him feel better immediately.

His frequent companion, who had not been invited to Elsie's, was napping on the couch and opened an eye now in trepidation. She hoped it wasn't going to be another one of those awful nights when he became hateful and sullen. Sometimes she wondered why she stayed with him. She'd thought of running away, but recognized a weakness in herself—a reluctance to be on her own. She liked being taken care of, and when he wasn't drinking he could be quite affectionate and generous. He was speaking to her now.

"Come on, kid," he said coolly, jiggling the car keys in his pocket. "Let's take a drive."

Obediently, she rose from the couch, and followed him.

Elsewhere in the building, nobody heard the sickening thud of Elsie's slump to the floor, the Plaza being practically soundproof. It was two nights and a day before she was missed.

Ordinarily, Christine Conrad, Elsie's across-the-hall neighbor, would have encountered her several times in the course of a day. But Christine was out of the country on a pleasure trip to Europe and would not be home for another week. And so Elsie lay, cold, stiff and still.

The night of her murder was, on the surface, much like any other balmy night in Burlingame. El Camino Real, literally "the King's Road," the main street through town and on which the Plaza fronted, was a very busy thoroughfare. It had been blazed by Indians and other converts through raw, rugged California by order of Franciscan friars over a period of fifteen years in the late 1770s. The road connected their twenty-one missions from San Diego in the south to Sonoma in the north. They'd named it for their patron, the king of Spain. Today, a major freeway, 101, roughly parallels it, extending all the way up the Pacific coast to the Canadian border.

Along the stretch of El Camino in Burlingame (nobody bothers with the "Real" anymore), a constant stream of local traffic moves. But the sounds hardly penetrated the steel and concrete walls of the Park Plaza Apartments. Tall, bushy eucalyptus trees lining the street further muffled the ceaseless noise.

Occasionally, the screech of brakes could be heard as a motorist played Russian roulette with the traffic lights. And now and then the night was split by the ear-piercing wail of an ambulance rushing to Mills or Peninsula Hospital. Such obtrusive sounds caused drapes to part in a few of the fifty-five apartments, as a curious tenant peered out. On the whole, though, the outlook was peaceful and quite magnificent.

Like sparkling fireflies, jet planes lit up the sky, coming in to land at San Francisco International Airport. To the south, the San Mateo Bridge spanning San Francisco Bay glittered like a chain of gold. To the north, the San Francisco skyline beckoned, its pinnacles and towers seeming, from a distance, mysterious, alluring, and exotic.

Monday night passed, and a new day dawned, and as it drew toward nine o'clock the coffee klatsch gathered in the lobby. This was a tradition among five of the older lady residents with plenty of time on their hands. It went on until nearly noon.

Laura Fiedler, the busty bustling manager, who lived in apartment 101 just behind her office, had begun "the klatsch" some years before as a way of getting the ladies out of her hair. Otherwise, they had a tendency to hang around her office, monopolizing her day. Over the years, however, Laura had come to enjoy the klatsches nearly as much as they did.

Although the decor of the lobby was on the garish side, pinks and purples with jungle green, it was comfortably furnished with plenty of armchairs and couches. And it always smelled good, for Laura diligently attacked it every day with scented lemon polish. It was a very convivial setting for sitting around and gossiping about the more newsworthy tenants. The daily obituaries were routinely scanned and discussed. At their ages, there usually was someone they knew.

To Plaza residents not participating, the chatter heard as they passed through the lobby sounded like buzzing bees.

"Did you hear that Ernie and Eva are divorcing?"

"No! Really? Tell me more!"

"Have you noticed how perky Mervin's been looking lately? They say he has a new lady friend."

"Oh, yes, I've seen her. She spends the night here quite often."

Such news would be confirmed or denied at noon when Don arrived. He was the mustached, husky, pigtailed mailman who deliberately made the Plaza his lunch hour stop so that he, too, could feel free to visit.

"Out of the way, now, ladies. Wait 'til I've finished sorting," he would scold good-naturedly. And when he was through putting the mail in the boxes (which never took long for he was surprisingly efficient), he would take a seat, open his sandwich, and join in.

"No, no, no, you've got that all wrong," he would say in his know-it-all manner, setting the ladies straight.

But even the coffee klatsch did not notice Elsie's absence, for she was not one of the "regulars."

And so Tuesday passed, and by Wednesday morning there was an accumulation of newspapers at Elsie's door—a *San Francisco Chronicle* from that morning and the day before, and last night's *San Mateo Times*. Clearly, something was wrong. It was the Scottie, Angus, who sounded the alarm.

Miffed by the lack of handouts the night before, Angus had parked outside 308. Pawing the papers and barking, he demanded that Elsie pay him his due.

Nancy, his owner, had stayed home from work that day, pleading her monthly period, an indulgence she allowed herself whenever she was feeling lazy. Engrossed in a phone chat, she was totally unaware of the ruckus Angus was making. His incessant barking was reported to the manager.

"That dog again. As if I didn't have anything else to do," muttered Laura. She slammed the phone in its cradle, and stomped to the elevator. Hitting the button, she rode to the third floor, indignantly "ssshhh"ing the dog's sharp barks as she charged down the long corridor.

Upon reaching 308, however, and seeing the stack of newspapers, a puzzled expression crossed her face. "That's strange," she said aloud.

She pushed the doorbell, but getting no response, reached in her pocket for the passkey. Angus, beside her, fell silent, his button eyes bright with anticipation.

"Excuse me!" Laura called out, entering apartment 308. "Mrs. Johnson? Are you here?"

Timorously, the manager went in. She was nervous about doing so, for Elsie was very uppity about her home being entered without permission. Laura knew there'd be hell to pay if the woman discovered her there.

The Scottie slipped in behind her and streaked across the room, barking hysterically.

Mechanically, reluctantly, with a chill sense of foreboding, Laura followed him—and abruptly stopped, looking down, aghast. "Oh, Mrs. Johnson!" she moaned, clapping a hand to her mouth.

Angus, excited by his benefactress lying so stiff and still, raced in mad circles around Elsie's body.

"Get out of here!" Laura shrieked, flailing at the dog with one of the folded newspapers.

"Annn-gussss!" came Nancy's call from down the hall.

The dog's ears perked up and he lit out for 302, dodging Laura's blows.

Laura was in shock. Nothing as traumatic as this had

ever happened in her manager jobs before. *What do I do now?* she wondered. *Phone the police? A doctor? My boss?* Instantly, she dismissed the last thought. She must not let her boss know she was not in control of the situation.

Right now, it was imperative to get out of there. The thought of using Elsie's phone made her feel sick. Besides, she'd watched enough TV dramas to know she shouldn't touch anything. By the time she descended to the sanity of her office, she'd recovered her wits. Why, of course. In any emergency, nine-one-one.

She dialed it, as she had so many times before, for in a building with some seventy-five tenants, calamity was no stranger. Heart attacks, seizures, cuts, burns, falls, even residents getting stuck in bathtubs were all part of life at the Plaza. This was the first time she'd called about a death, however.

Speaking into the telephone, her voice had trembled.

5
The Call

. . . Only three blocks away when she took the call, June Jacobs was the first to respond to the 911. Having lived in the small town all her life, she knew she'd create a commotion for it was very unusual for a police car to be called to the sedate Park Plaza.

Down the street at the Norsk Arms Apartments, it was a different story. Police were often summoned there to quell marital disputes and rowdy parties. But never the Plaza!

Importantly, June pulled alongside the red zone, backed and filled expertly, and stepped from the car, leaving Chief in the backseat until needed.

She was just seconds ahead of a public ambulance that careened off El Camino Real, siren whopping, wheels squealing. Two medics, a male and a female, hastily emerged and joined her. Right behind them, engine 14 of the Burlingame Fire Department screeched to a stop. Its husky young crew, sheathed in awkward, heavy brown and yellow jumpsuits, also leapt out, prepared to do their duty. Two more black and white police cars arrived, completing the spectacle.

Windows flew open as tenants peered out, and from all along the street other neighbors flocked from their buildings to cluster and watch with a compelling fascination to learn the news.

White-faced and tense, Laura Fiedler, the manager, opened the door. It seemed natural for June, having arrived first, to act as spokesperson for the group. "Hello," June said, softly and gently, hoping to put the woman at ease. "I'm Officer Jacobs. Will you show us what's happened, please?"

The gang of eight rode to the third floor together. Laura introduced herself along the way. "I'm sorry to be so shaky," she added. "This is a first experience for me."

June felt like confessing it was a "first" for her, too, but stifled the impulse.

Within the apartment, all was surprisingly neat, except for the pitifully dead white-haired woman lying so crumpled and still.

"Have you touched anything since you found her?" June asked Laura.

"Good Lord, no!" Laura replied.

"That's fine," June replied, relieved.

The medics looked up from their examination of the body. "No need to run a tape on her. She's dead all right," the head medic briskly announced. "And," he added, catching June's eyes, "it is not from natural causes." Discreetly, he nodded toward the fingerprint marks, by now purplish, around Elsie's neck.

Automatically, June reached for the two-way radio she wore at her hip that connected her with headquarters. "Investigations, please," she said, and explained the situation briefly. "We need a detective here."

"Detective?!" Laura reacted, incredulously. "Why do you need a detective? Didn't Mrs. Johnson probably just have a stroke and hit her head when she fell?" she asked June.

"It's just routine," June answered, soothingly choosing words that would not frighten the woman any more than she was already. "In a death of this sort," June explained, "we have to be sure no foul play was involved."

"*Foul* play?" echoed Laura. "You mean—murder?" Answering her own question, she moaned "Oh, my." Still in shock from viewing Elsie, Laura sank into the nearest chair.

This even closer proximity to the body, however—Elsie's eyes wide open and vacantly staring, her cupid's bow of a mouth frozen in a surprised "Oh"—caused Laura to spring to her feet again. "I've got to get out of here," Laura said, weakly.

June felt sorry for her. The woman was in for a lot more unpleasantness this day.

"Why don't you wait for the detective at your office?" she suggested.

Laura nodded weakly, and left, along with the medics and the firemen, who were no longer needed.

June remained behind with two of her fellow officers, observing what they could of the possible crime scene before more help arrived. For a moment, she felt a slight pang of guilt. Should she go down to the street and repark the police car, leaving the space free for her superior, the detective?

"Nah!" she decided. "I got here first."

In the lobby of the Plaza, the atmosphere was charged with tension. Apprehensive and curious, tenants crowded around Laura.

"What's going on?"

"I really don't know," Laura answered truthfully. "It's Elsie Johnson. She's dead."

"Dead? Elsie?!"

A disbelieving gasp as if from one voice swept the large room. Of all the unlikely people to die—Elsie, so haughty, so indomitable, so regal! From all sides, questions flew at Laura.

"Why didn't the medics take her away?"

"Why are the police still here?"

"What's this all about, anyway?"

Upset and confused, Laura snapped at them to go back to their own apartments, which no one had any intention of doing.

Instinctively, they huddled together, whispering, speculating among themselves, while Laura took refuge in her glassed-in office, locking the door behind her. Trembling with emotion and shock, she sat, elbows on the desk, hands cupping her head, vainly trying to hide from their stares.

6
Win

Some people take coffee breaks to relax. Sgt. Harry Winslow, detective with the Burlingame Police Department, liked to beat golf balls.

The range at the Crystal Springs Golf Course was only five minutes from his office, a straight shot uphill to the 280 freeway, then a left and a right onto Golf Course Drive.

Forty-one, with sandy hair, rugged features, and keen, kind green eyes, Win, as he liked to be called for short, had been under a lot of pressure lately. He had just finished solving a private home burglary case. The lady of the house had been cleaned out of all her old family silver. It was a situation she'd brought on herself by leaving a spiel on her answering machine about being out of town until the following Tuesday.

"Will they ever learn?" Win mused.

As usual, the paper work had been horrendous and a downer after the victory of locating the stash and capturing the thief. But he had gotten his culprit. He always did.

Win had felt a need to clear his head, and, as was his habit when he needed to get away, but not far, had escaped up the hill to the golf course. There he had let out his tensions by the sheer satisfaction, both mechanical and physical, of hitting a bucketful of balls.

He rarely had a chance to play, his job being so time-consuming and with an eighteen-hole game taking as long as four hours. On vacations, he made up for it, though, traveling places where he could play all day long if he liked. He had splurged the summer before on a golf package trip to Scotland and smiled now in memory at the sheer bliss it had been to play those wonderful old links courses—St. Andrews, Carnoustie, Turnberry.

To him, golf, even if only at a driving range, was a reviver to the spirit, calming to the soul. The sport never failed to refresh him with a new enthusiasm for his work, no matter how sordid it might turn out to be.

Golf was the quickest way he'd found to relax in his twenty years of police work. Even as a rookie cop in Winnetka, Illinois, he had practiced it. Upon moving to San Francisco and joining the force there, he had had to drop the sport, since there were no open-to-the-public ranges anywhere near the station. But now that he was assigned to the suburbs, the release of golf was again open to him.

Although some of his associates regarded him as a playboy for his infatuation with golf, most knew better. For Win's dedication to his work was at least as exacting as his addiction to the sport. A purposeful man with deceivingly plodding ways, he had successively solved every one of his cases to date, although he often took roundabout ways to do it. The call to report to the Park Plaza came just as he had hit the last of his thirty golf balls. It was a particularly well-struck five-iron that soared far, straight, and true.

"Be right there!" he acknowledged cheerfully into his pocket radio. He threw his clubs in the bag, and hurried to his car.

In five minutes, he was at the Plaza. Finding a police car where he had expected to park surprised him, but he was not one to pull rank and modestly cruised on down the block until finding an available space.

He parked, shrugged his sports jacket on, and walked

back to the Plaza. Ringing the bell, he courteously introduced himself to the manager, Laura. Big eyed and serious, she accompanied him to apartment 308.

"Do you need me anymore?" Laura asked, praying the answer would be no. She'd seen enough of Elsie's apartment that day to last her a lifetime.

"That's OK, ma'am. You may go." He smiled gently, appreciating her discomfiture. "We'll check with you before we leave."

Gratefully, Laura departed.

Entering 308, Win was momentarily diverted by the umbrella stand in the foyer holding the antique golf clubs. Reluctantly, he passed them by and stepped farther into the apartment.

The coroner, a doleful man of bland appearance, was busily working over the body. Win's detail men had also preceded him, and had fanned through the rooms, dusting for fingerprints, searching for clues.

Win smiled, delighted, upon seeing June. For three years now, he had been noticing her progress on the force, and how well she and the dog, Chief, worked together.

"Hi!" he said to her. "Haven't seen you for a while. How've you been?"

"Just fine, thanks," she answered, her sober face lighting up upon seeing him. Although she hardly knew him, he seemed so supportive. Always ready with an encouraging word and smile. He was her idol. Detective work was what she, too, hoped to work into one day.

"Will you be handling this investigation, sir?"

She was flustered, uncertain whether to call him by his proper name, Harry, or as "Win," the nickname she knew he preferred his co-workers to use. Both seemed a little familiar, so she compromised with the can't-go-wrong, respectful title of "Sir."

"I'm elected. And," he said sotto voce, so as not to offend the male officers, "I'll be needing a full-time helper. Are you interested if I can get you assigned to the case?"

"You bet!" she exclaimed.

"Great," he said. "Come on, then. Let's get started."

He ambled over to Elsie's body, and knelt to view it closely.

"Now, isn't this a shame. Poor lady," he muttered, noting the tell-tale marks on her throat.

The coroner, finished with his preliminary exam, rose to his feet and brusquely announced, "OK, boys, you can cover her up." To Win he said, "I'll try to have the autopsy report on your desk by tomorrow."

Win nodded his thanks.

Shielded at last from prying eyes, Elsie's shrouded body was lifted onto a gurney. The young male policemen formed a sort of honor guard as she was borne through the lobby.

News of her death had spread quickly. About a dozen residents stood around, gaping, morbidly curious.

"Please show Elsie some respect!" Laura wailed, wildly waving her hands.

Meanwhile, upstairs, Win's men had finished their initial search and had been given permission to leave. He and June were alone, now.

"There was no forced entry," June, who'd been inspecting the door lock, called out.

Her attention turned to a glass cabinet filled with curios in the corner, but the doors were neatly closed and, peering in, she saw nothing remiss. She turned away and went into the bedroom.

"There's a watch case on the bureau," she called out. "Nothing's in it."

"Hmmm, and she wasn't wearing a watch," Win reacted, jotting the fact in his notepad.

"Well, we know when it happened," he said a moment later. From the coffee table, he had picked up a *San Mateo Times* still in its wrapping, dated two nights before.

"And she was obviously on good terms with her visitor," he added, noting the two drinking glasses nearby, full of now stale and vile-smelling whiskey.

Irresistibly, as he moved to the door and passed the umbrella stand, he reached out and reverently touched the blade of one of the old golf clubs. A track iron, he guessed. Strange that an elderly lady, who didn't look at all athletic, would want to own such things. Putting his mind back on business, he told June, "There's nothing more we can do in here today. Let's seal up."

As the last person out, June fixed the customary sticker to the doorjamb, symbolically protecting the death scene from being intruded upon. It was the first time she'd handled one, and it struck her as strange for such an important notice to be so small.

"Well," Win sighed to June outside of door 308, "this is a large building and the day is young. Let's start collecting statements.

"I'll take this floor and five and six. You do the others. Better take the dog with you. It's Chief, right?"

"Yes, sir," she acknowledged.

He shook his head, wryly. "Don't bother with that 'sir' stuff. I'm 'Win' to you, okay?"

"Yes, sir," she responded, again from habit. "I mean Win," she giggled, correcting herself.

"Oh, and another thing," he told her. "You can hang your uniform in the closet when you get home tonight. I'd like you to work in civilian clothes. That way, the people here should feel easier around us. That all right with you?"

"Fine!" she responded, although secretly she was disappointed for she enjoyed the instant respect the uniform gave her.

"And don't take my parking space anymore, OK?" he added, teasingly.

She flushed in embarrassment at her goof.

As ordered, June took the elevator to the street level and went to the car to get her partner Chief. Smartly, he leapt to the sidewalk and stood waiting for the click of his leash. They reentered the Plaza, he padding proudly at her side.

Tenants lingering in the lobby looked askance and nervously at this unusual team. Small dogs in the Plaza were nothing new, but a *police* dog! Well!

Knocking on fifty-five doors to get statements consumed all the rest of that day, and a good part of the evening.

"Pardon me, sir, (or madam)," was heard up and down the corridors on every floor. "May I have a word with you?"

Win took the third, fifth, and sixth floors.

The dog, Chief, stood tall and dignified beside June, his intelligent, unblinking brown eyes calmly searching the truth from everybody she interviewed on floors one, two, and four.

7
Inner Circle

"May I come in?" June asked the diminutive Chinese who answered her knock at apartment 108.

"Please," Mr. Chin replied, standing aside politely so that she might enter.

"What a beautiful Shih-Tzu!" she exclaimed, seeing the silky smooth dog reclined on the sofa, its back legs stretched impossibly straight out behind.

The Shih-Tzu stared inscrutably at Chief, totally ignoring June and her compliment.

"Meet Ming," Mr. Chin beamed.

The dog was his proudest possession, next to his wife and child, of course.

Mr. Chin was one of those rare persons, born and bred in San Francisco. His grandfather had been a coolie, cheap labor imported from China in the 1860s to hand hammer the last few hundred miles of track of transcontinental railroad. When the work was completed, he had gravitated to San Francisco's fast growing Chinatown and married. Their son, Mr. Chin's father, had opened a modest restaurant, which he and his wife had operated during their lifetime together.

Tommy, as he'd been known in his youth, had grown up helping in the restaurant after school. And when his parents died, he, the only child, then twenty, took it over.

From that day on, he elected to be known as "Mr. Chin." He had devoted full energy to his work. Over the years his restaurant, not fancy but fine, had become one of the city's "in" spots among devotees of excellent and inexpensive Chinese cuisine.

For years, Mr. Chin had skimped on himself, living in unfashionable neighborhoods, plowing much of his profit back into the restaurant. But he had also banked and invested considerable savings. Finally, at sixty, he decided it was time to retire, sell the restaurant, and enjoy himself.

He hungered to know more about the country of his heritage. And so he had traveled to China, to see for himself the Ming Tombs, the Great Wall, the Forbidden City. Finished with sightseeing, he ventured to the peasant village where his grandparents had been born. There he met a young woman. At least, being only thirty, she seemed very young to him.

He became enchanted with her. She was eager to leave China and improve her lot in life. They made an arrangement. They would marry; she need not sleep with him as long as she promised to keep him company the rest of his natural life.

As a married couple, they returned to San Francisco and after several months moved south to Burlingame, where the rents were considerably cheaper than what he'd been paying on Clay Street. In the more relaxed climate of the suburbs, Mr. Chin and his young wife became lovers, and, incredibly at his age, parents. A beautiful girl child had been born to them. Now six, she dutifully clung to their hands while being escorted to school.

All that was missing in Mr. Chin's belated domestic life was a dog. He had always wanted one, but it was a luxury he had never felt he could afford. Now he could relax the purse strings. His investments were doing very nicely indeed. If he could afford to have a wife and child, he could certainly indulge himself with a dog. He liked the leonine looks and the calm meditative ways of the Shih-Tzu. Such a superior being. Just like him!

Exceedingly polite, Mr. Chin was one of the rare men at the Plaza who would stand back, with a hint of a smile and a small formal bow, to let his wife, daughter, dog, and any other women who happened to be around, out the door first. But to June he seemed oddly evasive, as she questioned him about Monday.

"So sorry," he said, "I saw nothing."

"What about your neighbor across the hall?" she pressed. "Did you see him that night?" She was curious to know his answer, for she had already called on Mr. Allen and felt a glimmer of suspicion toward him for his overly hearty demeanor.

"So sorry," Mr. Ming repeated. "Mr. Allen is a very loud man. We usually know when he is home. But Monday?" He pursed his thin lips in thought. "No, I did not hear him. Or see him. So sorry."

June thanked him for his time. He bowed.

As she and Chief prepared to leave, she noticed that the Shih-Tzu had not moved an iota but was now sticking out its perfect pink tongue at her. With a human, the gesture would have been insulting. From a Shih-Tzu, however, it was a compliment. June knew it meant he felt comfortable with her.

Finding a police gal at his door was quite unnerving to Bob Delaware of apartment 210. He'd never liked assertive women. His first impulse when he saw the uniform was to shut the door in her face, after some polite excuse of course. But what the heck, she was pretty. This could be amusing. Might as well turn on the old charm, he thought.

He had a great smile, and it came across as natural when his apricot standard poodle, Gigi, gamboled forward to greet the shepherd. "Looks like my dog wants to meet yours!" Bob said lightly, ushering her in.

June laughed. *Attractive guy,* she mused. *Good build. Becoming skin tones of a person who spends a lot of time outdoors.* He appeared to be about forty-five. *Wonder if he's single?* Well, she would soon find out.

"I need to ask a few questions," she began.

"Shoot," he said, hands in his pockets, amiably casual.

"There was some trouble in this building the other night."

"Oh?" He raised an eyebrow. "I hadn't heard. What about?"

"It involved Mrs. Johnson on the floor above you."

"Oh, yeah," he responded, "I know who you mean. Nice old lady."

"She's dead."

"No!"

He looked, June thought, honestly horrified. She hastened to soften the news. "It may have been an accident. We're trying to reconstruct what happened. Were you home Monday evening?"

"Yuh, right here," he said. "Locked up on a story," he elaborated.

She looked confused.

"No write, no eat," he said.

She looked interested, so he told her something of his life as a freelance golf writer.

How refreshing. A modest man! she thought, as he kidded about barely eking out a living writing golf articles for various newspapers and magazines.

What she didn't know was he was telling the truth. At from $500 to $2,000 per story sold, and maybe two sales a month if he was having a good month, his writing income was far from sensational and definitely erratic. It did, however, have its perks. Like free green fees wherever he wanted to play and occasional press trips to expensive golf resorts.

June was eager to get him back on track and also wanted to learn more about him. "Maybe your wife heard something the other night?" she asked.

"I'm not married," he told her.

He had been, when he'd moved into the Plaza five years before. But he saw no reason to bring that up. Sure, he had resented his wife making more money than he. What guy wouldn't? So he hadn't been the easiest person in the world to get along with. So what! That was history.

The poodle, Gigi, had been bought by his wife to serve as a balm to the troubled marriage. But expecting a dog to be a solution to their problems had not worked, and when his wife moved out she'd left Gigi behind, wanting no reminders of the unhappy alliance. Bob had stayed on at the Plaza, keeping the same apartment but fixing up the bedroom to serve also as an office.

He was doing better now as a writer, far more productive since learning to use a computer. The words fairly leapt from his fingers now, his imagination unleashed with the freedom of silent creation. He had an extensive collection of golf reference books, and often found inspiration from articles in them. But playing the game was what he loved most of all and did on the slightest whim.

As they talked, June thought it peculiar that not once, after Delaware's first pleasant remark at the door, did he again acknowledge his dog. She shoved that impression to the back of her mind.

Guess he's just not feeling demonstrative today, she thought.

She walked to the door, and he opened it for her.

"See you again?" he asked, with an engaging grin and a flirtatious wink.

She was careful to give a cool, professional tone to her double-meaning answer. "Yes, I expect we will."

"Am I getting paranoid? I must be slipping," June said to herself. "Why can't I get through to this person?"

She was on the fourth floor now, near the end of her rounds, and had just met George Schmidt and his plump dachshund, Hans, in apartment 404.

The man had glossy brown, almost-red hair, plastered close to his head in an old-fashioned, parted-in-the-middle style. Age about fifty. The odd thing about him was he would not meet her eyes. Was it her imagination or did he seem furtive, looking everywhere but at her?

George, who had an unconscious habit of ducking his head when talking with a woman, was thinking, *I wish I could tell her how shy she makes me feel. She is so direct; so sure of herself. I want to be cooperative, but I don't like people coming to my door unannounced. Why couldn't she have phoned first?* He shuffled his feet, and hung his head, and looked to his dog for support. The dachshund, however, seemed happy to have the visitors. If dogs could salute, Hans certainly would have, in respect to the big German shepherd.

Noticing Hans's rapt expression, a faint smile crossed George's face for he, too, had an inbred pride for all things German. He'd been born in Milwaukee of parents who, although American citizens, insisted on speaking German at home. After his parents died, a vague stirring for adventure had lured him West. Although he usually found cities intimidating, he had been drawn to San Francisco. But his life was empty there. He had no friends, no hobbies. Just went to work, came home. Every day the same.

One day off, just for "something different" to do, he had ridden the train from San Francisco to San Jose, and thus discovered Burlingame. On the spur of the moment, he had climbed off the train, walked about, and liked what he saw. The next day he gave notice at his dreary apartment in the Mission district and quit his job selling watches at Macy's.

In Burlingame, he had seen a sign outside the Park Plaza Apartments that made his heart leap. "Pets Welcome" it said. He had always wanted a dog.

Yes, they had a vacancy. He went directly to a pet shop and bought Hans. They moved to the Plaza together. Although a loner, and not prone to let happiness or otherwise show on his face, George was as satisfied now as he had ever been.

A bachelor, he had never married, never having met "the right woman"—or never having the nerve to pop the question. A meticulous man, and a talented tinkerer, he loved to take mechanical things apart and reassemble them better than ever. He had a fine collection of classical music CDs and the best sound system in the building, which he himself had designed. He had a respectable job as a watch repairman at a jewelry shop on Burlingame Avenue. He was so devoted to it that he often brought repair work home with him. The shop was just two easy walking blocks from the Plaza. Who could ask for a better commute!

Best of all, George had Hans. To him, the dog was like a little brother. He kept Hans sleek and shining, played with him, talked to him, loved him so much he would even sprint home on his coffee breaks to enjoy him as much as possible.

Could a man like this ever feel deeply? June wondered as she talked with him. *Or is he destined to be a wimp?* "Are you sure you noticed nothing unusual around the building on Monday?" She had to say it a second time. Really! The man was so dense!

"Nothing, ma'am," George answered, eyes darting wildly.

It was a fib. He *had* noticed some unusual activity Monday night, but as it couldn't possibly have anything to do with the death in 308, he decided to keep his mouth shut. He didn't want to get his lovely friend, Mimi, on the sixth floor, in trouble. And also, with a pang, he recalled an involvement of his own with Elsie that might prove a problem. He blanched at the thought.

June noticed.

"Are you all right, Mr. Schmidt?" she said, concerned. He had looked for a moment as if he might faint.

"I'm fine," he said, forcing himself at last to meet her eyes.

They were nice eyes, she observed, surprised. Clear, brown, honest.

"Is there anything else you'd like to tell me?" she urged.

"No, ma'am," he said, decisively.

8
Rest of the Pack

"So this is Angus. You're a smart little feller, aren't you?" Win said, stooping to pat the Scottie upon being admitted into apartment 302, Nancy Webb's home. The friendly little dog preened at the attention, cocking his head in curiosity as to who this stranger was.

Rising from his crouching position, Win couldn't help but notice Nancy's physical attributes, starting with her splendid legs. She was barefoot, in shorts and clinging T-shirt, her favorite garb when not going to work. (Her working wardrobe was an eye-catcher, too, always looked forward to by male residents of the town and commuters on the train to and from San Francisco. She favored three-inch heels and short skirts, a dynamite combination.)

The top half of her was in perfect proportion to the bottom, and her face was a knockout. She was, he guessed, about twenty-five. (Actually he was ten years off. Nancy looked far younger than her true thirty-five.)

She shot him a ravishing smile. It was always gratifying to her to receive admiring glances.

Wonder where he's from? she thought, not quite able to place his faint accent.

She, herself, had not entirely lost her tell-tale twang from Pittsburgh, Pennsylvania, although she had left there at twenty-two. She had come as far West as her money allowed, anxious to carve a new life for herself following the end of a love affair.

In San Francisco, her good looks and capable ways had helped her find a pleasant job as girl friday for an architectural firm. With the job came a plus. Although she was expected to be at work by 8:00 a.m., they closed the office at 4:00. This was fine all during her twenties. With an extra couple of daylight hours, she could more fully enjoy her garden apartment on Green Street.

She joined the California Tennis Club and made a point of making dates for late afternoon games and lessons. It was an amiable easygoing way of existence, but when Nancy turned thirty, and faced the likelihood of remaining single, she realized she was lonely.

"I need someone to love and love me back. What do I do about this?" she confronted herself. Flipping through the newspaper, she had noticed an ad for the annual San Francisco Dog Show. It would take place soon at the large convention hall south of town facetiously called the Cow Palace because, once a year, it hosted a rodeo.

"That's it! I'll get a dog for company!" she told herself. She attended the dog show and browsed the halls until finding a breed that suited her. The Scottie appealed for its cocky, comical, and responsive ways. And so Angus had come into her life.

Dogs not being allowed at her Green Street apartment, she had to move. That was no hardship. She'd grown tired of frenetic city living, anyway. However, she kept her job. She liked being the one woman in the office, was fond of the men, loved the pay.

Moving to Burlingame and commuting to work suited her fine. She was an early riser, so walking Angus around the block at daybreak was no problem. She still had ample time for breakfast and to catch the 7:21.

At the Plaza, Nancy had become good friends with another dog owner of about her same age. Ruth Kenny, a librarian for the city of Burlingame, came home for lunch every day and to walk her cute mutt, Millie. When Ruth volunteered to take Angus on the noon walks, too, Nancy gratefully accepted and gave her a duplicate key to 302. Since Nancy was always home before dark, her pet was never alone for too long. And besides, she left the radio on for his entertainment.

Nancy adored her apartment. Most of the time, when she was home, she didn't even bother to lock her door. At least, not until now. Why? What's there to fear? she had reasoned before today. Even if there were, Angus would alert her.

No, she hadn't noticed anything unusual on Monday, she told Win. Angus had even enjoyed his paper game with Elsie Johnson that night.

"And what time was *that?*" Win asked.

"About five, just like always. Poor little guy. He's been pining for her ever since."

Working his way along the fifth floor, Win was perplexed by the skittery lady in 507. He prided himself on his nonthreatening appearance and yet just the mere fact of his being a man seemed to terrorize Miss Stella Rankin. She reminded him of a frightened, wounded bird. She wouldn't let him in. He had to be content with talking through a three-inch length of chain, and he had to strain to hear her replies to his questions, for she spoke in whispers.

There being no reason to pursue her any further, he bid her good-bye. As he left her door, he heard the latch lock and the chain click back in place and a third lock turned.

"Boy!" he said to himself. "That lady is some scared cookie!"

The next tenant was a pleasant relief. Ruth Kenny in apartment 503 reminded Win of the actress Katharine Hepburn in her prime. Tall and thin, with angular features and a sharp way of speaking, she had a sophisticated crispness about her. To many residents of the Plaza, this made her alliance with Millie, a mongrel, seem strange. But Nancy, Ruth's closest friend, understood the bonds between the two.

Like her pet, which she'd adopted from the Peninsula Humane Society, Ruth was a survivor who had risen above a bad beginning, neglected and abused as a youth. She never spoke of her parents anymore, nor of her girlhood in Boston. It had taken her a long time to learn to smile and trust people. Like Nancy, she had escaped her past by moving to California, first to Los Angeles, then to Pasadena, a town eminently more to her liking. She had gone to college there and graduated with a degree in library science.

It was a job opening at the Burlingame Public Library that had brought her to this small, attractive, northern California town, where she hoped she could live forever. Bad dreams, bad memories, were behind her now. She loved books, and their fountain of knowledge. Her favorite TV show was "Jeopardy." She was gleeful that she could often outwit the contestants.

She was a superb librarian. With an interesting career, a place in the community, her dog Millie for a loyal companion, and Nancy for best friend, Ruth considered her life quite full.

She and Nancy were well aware that many residents believed they were gay. They didn't care. They honestly were "just friends." Once a week, however, just to give the old biddies in the building something to gossip about, they would go out for dinner in the town, linking arms defiantly as they swept through the lobby in a public show of their affection for each other.

"We dined out on Monday," she told Win.

That's funny, he thought. *Wonder why Nancy Webb didn't mention it?*

"What time?" he asked, perfunctorily.

"About seven," she answered.

"Did you notice anything at all different around the building that night?" he asked.

"Not a thing," she breezily answered.

In the back of her mind, there *was* a nagging memory. As she and Nancy had passed in front of the garage on their way to dinner Monday evening, they had had to jump out of the way of a car that had come tearing out in one hell of a hurry. It had seemed to be a couple; the passenger had long curly hair. But neither Nancy nor she had gotten a clear look, and as that sort of nuisance happened fairly often, Ruth deemed it insignificant, not worth mentioning.

Her funny little clown-faced Millie had been sitting quietly, seemingly listening to the conversation. Suddenly the dog rolled over on its back, exposing its vulnerable belly. Ruth laughed, embarrassed by the dog's wantonness at giving the traditional female sign of surrender.

"Don't worry. I believe her," Win told Millie, giving a wink to Ruth.

"Ah! Things are looking up!" Win said to himself. Apartment 605 had just responded to his pushing of the bell, and he was meeting Mimi Masterson. A flaming redhead with a come-hither smile and a husky voice, she ushered him into her living room. Or was it a boudoir? An enormous king-sized bed dominated the living room. The bed was covered by numerous fluffy sheepskins that had been stitched together as one. A menagerie of toy animals were piled against the bolster pillows.

Tossing a grinning crocodile aside, Mimi motioned to Win to sit. "What can I do for you, officer?"

He posed his standard question, was satisfied with the answer, and although she made it clear he need not leave so soon, he did.

Smothering a smile at the surprise of Mimi, Win paid his last call to apartment 608. Helen Emmons, a twittery widow in her seventies, lived there with her black cocker spaniel, Pepper. As an elderly lady, Helen was short and dumpy, but in her dimpled youth, back in Atlanta, Georgia, she'd been the belle of many a ball and wasn't about to let anyone forget it.

She had carried into adulthood many of the flirtatious ways of her youth. Her tinkling laugh and batting eyelashes struck some of the Plaza's tenants as silly. But she was good-natured, and kind, and Pepper, wide-mouthed face fixed in perpetual smile, played up to her vanity, letting her know she was lovely.

Helen thrived on people. She was a chatterbox, and never missed the companionship of the coffee klatsch. She had a married son, who lived in Menlo Park, farther down the peninsula, and a married daughter across the Golden Gate Bridge in Tiburon. Both of them elected to stay at a distance.

A grandmother of six, Helen lavished attention on everybody, even the in-laws. She could be overwhelming in her craving for affection, both giving of and taking from. Long ago, she had exhausted her husband. She lived on his generous life insurance. She could well afford a condominium, or even a house, but apartment living suited her people needs better. Like Elsie Johnson, Helen found it stimulating to have friends of many different ages and backgrounds.

She had not only out-lived her husband, but also her beloved first dog. She had coped with the husband's death, but nearly had a nervous breakdown over losing the pet. Her doctor had bought her the spaniel Pepper as a therapeutic gift, she told Win. The placid, loving animal had given her a reason for getting up every morning.

"Pepper and I know everything that's going on in this building," Helen bragged, with a smirk.

"Oh?" Win responded.

"Yes, indeed," she droned. "We get a lot of exercise riding up and down in the elevator. My little dog is so smart. You should see her counting the floors. She feels the vibrations of the cables through her pads. She always knows exactly where we are. Isn't that clever?" Pepper, long, fringed ears listening, seemed to cringe at the gushiness of her mistress's voice.

"Oh yes, ma'am." Win tactfully replied. "That's a real intelligent dog you've got there.

"What a waste of time that was," he muttered to himself as he left.

And yet, he pondered, maybe not. These innocuous-seeming preliminaries before the serious business of sleuthing began were the part of the job he liked best. He looked upon the interlude as a cat-and-mouse game, with the hunter and hunted equals so far.

9
Desk Set

At the police station Friday morning, Win and June were huddled at his desk, comparing notes from their interviews. The dog, Chief, lay snoozing at June's feet. Win had ordered the desk sergeant not to put through any incoming calls. "Fend them off," Win had said. "Give any excuse. We need to concentrate."

The phone rang in the other room. June listened as the officer on duty, a matronly lady brisk in gold badge and blue uniform, snapped into the mouthpiece, "He's working the street. Is there a message?"

June laughed, amused by the common expression the clerk had used. "I hope she never says that about me!" she remarked to Win. "Sounds like a street walker!"

"Hmmmmm?" Win had barely heard her, engrossed in sorting his notes.

"Nothing," she sighed.

"OK." He was in gear now, and looked at her brightly. "Who've we missed?" Laura had given him a list of tenants' names that corresponded to the apartment numbers. He laid it on the desk.

"No contact yet with 307," June reported.

"She's in Europe," Win rebutted, dismissing Christine Conrad. "Who else have you not yet talked with?"

"401," she replied, consulting her notes. "Laura said he's on a business trip. Oh, and 408," she added.

"Leon Levin," Win mused, running down the names.

"He seems to be quite evasive," June mentioned. "I've tried his door three times."

"We'll catch him this morning," Win declared.

His own phone was ringing now. He looked to the anteroom in annoyance at the interruption, but the clerk merely shrugged, mouthing the words, "It's the coroner!"

"Good!" Win acknowledged with a smile and a wave, picking up the receiver.

"Boy, that was fast!" he said to the coroner.

"Yeah," he heard. "Yesterday was a slow day for deaths in Burlingame so I was able to get right on the Johnson autopsy."

"And what did you find out?" Win asked. "Oh, yeah?" he reacted.

"You don't say! . . ."

"Really? . . ."

"Thanks!"

Win hung up and said to June, "That's it, then."

"That's what?"

"The coroner's report on Mrs. Johnson. It's a homicide for sure. She died of a massive hemorrhage in her brain, no doubt caused by striking her head as she fell. And why did she fall? The marks around her neck are a dead giveaway. Let's go," he said rising.

Chief sprang to his feet in response. June stood also. "To the Plaza?" she queried.

"You've got it."

"We'll take my car," he said in the parking lot. "You want to drive?"

"Is that a request or an order?" she said, saucily.

"What do you think?" he smiled.

"Give me the keys!" she laughed.

Chief jumped into the backseat, and they were off.

10
The Baker

Merv Allen in apartment 105 frowned. He hated these jobs-for-hire. The calls always came at an inconvenient time, just when he was feeling his most creative. Maybe, soon, he wouldn't have to do them any more. He hung up the phone and pattered barefoot to the kitchen, his flapping bathrobe sashed loosely around his enormous girth.

He'd baked two loaves of bread earlier and had set them aside to cool. He grabbed a sharp knife and sliced into one. He stuffed a piece in his mouth and critically savoured it. *Not quite right,* he thought, disappointed. *Almost, but not quite. I'll try again tomorrow.*

He placed the remainder of the loaf in the refrigerator, wrapped the second one in foil, and left it on the counter while he went to his bedroom to change to his uniform of part-time security guard.

With some effort, he succeeded in buttoning the jacket around his mammoth stomach. He glanced in the mirror to assure himself that his badge was on straight. Adjusting his cap to a more rakish angle, he grinned at his image. Pausing in the kitchen, he picked up the wrapped bread and left the apartment.

The opening of Merv's door released the warm yeasty scent of the baking. It wafted down the hall and beneath the threshold of the Chin's apartment.

The Shih-Tzu caught the aroma first, and twitched its squat nose appreciatively. Mr. Chin smelled it, too. As a longtime restaurateur, it brought back happy memories. "Ah, sourdough!" he exclaimed to his smiling wife.

"I guess we can expect another visit from Mr. Allen soon. His recipe is still not perfect, but almost. Maybe this time I won't turn him down."

Mrs. Chin nodded, approvingly.

Merv swung down the hall, as light-footed as it was possible for a man of his six-foot four-inch height and three-hundred-pound weight to be.

The door to Laura's office was open. She was talking with the detective and the policewoman whom Merv couldn't help but leer at. She was quite a dish out of uniform, blond hair falling free, body clothed becomingly in beige sweater and slacks. Pausing at the doorsill, he thrust the loaf of bread at Laura. "A present!" he announced, flippantly.

"Thanks!" she said, looking up and smiling.

He tipped his cap smartly, and went to his job.

"He's buttering me up. Probably going to be late with his rent again this month," Laura told her visitors.

Win and June chuckled and exchanged glances at each other. Each wondered why Merv should be habitually late with his rent. If he had a financial problem, might it have something to do with the demise of wealthy Elsie Johnson? So many tenants. So many characters. The plot was thickening, just the way Win liked it.

11
On His Toes

As Merv made his exit out the double door, the "Enter" side opened with a deft, sure touch. "Speaking of the devil, there he is now!" Laura said to the police officers. Before Merv's interruption, Win and June had been questioning her about the resident of 408.

Laura had told them of his habit of taking a morning walk. "And another walk at noon. And one in the evening. I could time my watch by him. He should be back at any moment." And now he had returned, this tenant whom June had found so illusive.

Win rose to his feet and intercepted the man.

"Good morning, sir. You are Leon Levin?"

A slim, dapper man, beautifully garbed in suit, vest, and tie—with the incongruous footwear of tennis shoes—Levin stopped and, posturing his walking stick, allowed that he was.

June stepped forward also, with the dog Chief at her side. "I'm Sergeant Winslow, Burlingame Police," Win said. "This is Officer Jacobs. May we have a word with you, please?"

"Certainly," said Leon Levin.

Win headed for the lobby lounge area, expecting the others to follow, but as the ladies of the klatsch were beginning to assemble, that meeting place was clearly out. "Mind if we talk in your apartment?" Win asked.

Levin raised his eyebrow and nonchalantly adjusted a red carnation in the buttonhole of his handsome jacket.

"It's a private matter," Win explained. "Strictly routine. But we do need to ask some personal questions."

"Of course," Levin agreed, twirling his stick in a debonair manner.

As they stepped into the elevator and were about to ride up, a voice called out, "Hold it!"

June held her finger on the "Door Open" switch while George Schmidt entered with his dachshund.

"It's four, right?" June said with a friendly smile to the man who had seemed so timid at their brief meeting the day before.

George nodded tensely and stood stiffly before them. The plump little dachshund cautiously edged away from Levin's toe-tapping foot, beneath the protection of Chief's long legs.

As they rode up, Win studied the elusive Mr. Levin. He was certainly a distinguished-looking gent, Win thought. With his head of silver hair and rakish moustache trimmed pencil-thin, he appeared to be about seventy. For sake of conversation, Win commented, "Nice walking stick you have there."

"Thank you. It's one of my favorites," Levin acknowledged. He released his hold to show the grip to the detective.

"My God! It's a golf club! A mashie niblick, isn't it?" Win exclaimed.

"I believe that's what it's called," Levin answered loftily. "I played a bit of golf in my youth. Some of these older clubs make marvelous walking sticks. Used upside down, of course. Better than canes. Stronger.

"I find this one particularly effective for shooing away small boys riding bicycles on the sidewalk," Levin cackled.

"Well, it's a beauty," Win said, dumbfounded, examining the old stick. "Where did you ever find it?"

"It was a present," Levin answered, airily.

They were at the fourth floor now. Silent George and his dog turned one way, Levin and the police team the other.

Inside apartment 408, the visitors looked about admiringly. Levin's home was a decorator's dream, subtly disciplined in its display of possessions. And it was a fascinating, eclectic mix.

A priest's ceremonial robe, grandly framed, took up most of one wall, its satin and velvet sleeves outstretched in benediction. There were many photographs on another wall of Levin with various lady friends. Featured prominently was Elsie Johnson.

"You wanted to ask me something?" Levin said, breaking their reverie.

"Yes, we do," said Win. "You were acquainted with Mrs. Elsie Johnson?"

"I was indeed," said Levin. "A most lovely lady."

"Did you happen to see her last Monday?"

"Not that *night*," Levin answered.

Win picked up on Levin's knowledge of Elsie's death having happened in the evening. But rumors, he realized, were running rampant through the building, and the fact that an investigation was in progress was hardly news.

With an easy-seeming aplomb, Levin added, "She was a very dear friend. We had visited earlier in the day over luncheon at Aquaterra." It was the newest "in" restaurant in town.

The conviviality of their last visit was embedded in Levin's mind for he had had great admiration for Elsie. They had shared a great many interests: books, art, theater, ballet. And they had discussed all of them at lunch that day in a nonstop talking marathon. As always, they had left much unsaid, and he had looked forward to picking up the threads of their conversation when next he saw her.

"I miss her very much," Levin said. "What a shame for this unfortunate accident to have happened." He bit his lip bravely, but to his puzzlement the detective seemed not to notice.

Win walked across the room and opened the living room window. He looked down. "Mrs. Johnson's apartment is directly below yours, isn't it?" Win asked.

"Why, yes," Levin answered.

"But you say you heard nothing from down there on Monday night?" Win pressed. "No shouts? No loud voices? Sounds *do* rise, you know."

"Sergeant," Levin replied, waspishly. "As I have already told you, I heard nothing at all from downstairs. Absolutely nothing. I am devastated by Elsie's death. She was a very dear friend."

"I'm sorry for your loss, sir," Win said, nodding to June that they should leave. "Thank you for your time."

Outside in the corridor, June looked at Win quizzically. "You believe him?" she asked.

"Yuh, to a point," Win said, thoughtfully rubbing his chin. "Meet me at 308 in a few minutes, will you?"

"Okay," she agreed, wondering what he was up to and why she wasn't being included.

12
Self-Winding

"Damn it," George muttered, letting himself into apartment 404. "She's done it again," she being the policeperson he had just been with in the elevator, and it meaning his awkwardness in her presence. But seeing her had reminded him of something he had to do. He went to his dresser, opened the top drawer, and removed a gleaming, shimmering object. He would ask advice of his good friend Mimi.

Telling Hans to "stay and be good," George went to the elevator and pushed the ascending button. It came and he stepped in, punching 6. He was so deep in thought of his problem that he didn't see Helen Emmons until she spoke to him.

"Going the wrong way, aren't you, George?" She had felt the slack tighten on her leash as her spaniel looked up for a reason to this interruption at 4 of the counting-the-floors routine.

George sheepishly smiled for an answer, and when they reached 6 and separated, she watched curiously as he knocked on the door of 605, Mimi's place. "Hi, George!" was the end of Helen Emmons' observation, as a bare, slim arm pulled him inside.

Mimi never put on her sexy routine when with her friend George. With him, she was completely herself—no phony act, no screwy ways. George was the best friend she had in the building. Hell! Probably the *only* friend! She chuckled.

Let alone the fact that he had saved her hundreds of dollars by fine-tuning her TV, setting up her music system, and fixing anything else electrical that she asked him to do, she liked him. *Really* liked him. And when his hair was ruffled and his collar undone the way he was now, she found him very appealing.

"What can I do for you, George?" she asked.

"I need advice, Mimi." He looked at her, pleadingly.

"Sure, if I can," she offered, shrugging a shoulder. "What about?"

"This." He drew from his pocket a beautiful Baume and Mercier gold link bracelet watch and showed it to her. Its bevel glittered with diamonds, its mother-of-pearl dial glowed. It reeked expensive.

"*Very* nice," she appreciated. "But what's the problem?"

"It's Elsie Johnson's."

"Oh," she reacted, assuming he'd stolen it.

He read the meaning in her eyes, and hastened to explain.

"It wasn't running right. Can you believe she dropped it in the tub? She brought it to me for repair. She was insistent about having it back quickly. You know how she was?"

Mimi nodded grimly, knowing all too well how difficult it was saying no to Elsie.

"So I brought the watch home to work on," George continued. "It's running fine now. I was going to give it back to her Tuesday, and then all this happened."

"So what's the problem?" Mimi said. "Why don't you just keep it?"

"I can't do that," he said, shocked at her presumptuousness. "I want to return it, but who can I give it to?" he asked her.

"Why don't you just leave it in an envelope at her door?" she suggested.

"No," he said, shaking his head. "Can't do that. It's worth sixteen thousand!"

"But George," Mimi reminded him. "You can get inside her apartment. You have a key, remember? You could just slip in and leave the watch in some conspicuous place."

George slapped his forehead, mockly scolding his memory. "I forgot about the key," he said, relieved. "Thanks, Mimi. That's what I'll do."

"Be careful," she told him. "Don't let anyone see you."

"You'd better be careful, too," he said as he turned to leave. "I saw you on Monday, coming in with that guy who stayed so long."

"Why, George!" she teased. "I didn't know you cared!"

George walked the three flights down, not wanting to chance another elevator encounter with a nosy neighbor. He looked to see if the coast was clear. It was, so he bent to the door of 308. The "stay away" sticker had been removed, he noticed gratefully.

He opened the door and, stepping inside, found the watch case on Elsie's bureau. He placed the watch carefully on its bed of white velvet. Retracing his steps, he closed the door behind him and had just turned for the stairs when he heard his name called.

"Wait right there, Mr. Schmidt!" the policewoman was calling. She had just stepped from the elevator.

Feeling sick at the pit of his stomach, George waited stoically for her approach. She had the dog, Chief, on alert, stiffly staring him down.

"Would you like to explain what you're doing here?" June said, reaching his side.

He nodded, swallowing hard.

"We can talk better inside," she offered, leading him by the elbow back into Elsie's apartment.

"So, how did you happen to have a key?" June demanded.

George told her. "Mrs. Johnson gave it to me months ago. She said it would give her peace of mind to have a network of friends around the building who could come to her rescue in case she ever needed help."

"You mean, there are *other* people who have keys to this apartment?" June asked, incredulously.

"I believe so."

"Who?"

"I don't know," he said, befuddled and anxious to be out of there.

This guy's just naive enough to be telling the truth, June decided, so she told him she believed him and that he was free to go. "And Mr. Schmidt," she added, in a softer tone of voice. "You were right to return the watch."

He smiled with relief and stood a lot straighter. And she realized, with a start, why, he wasn't a wimp at all.

13
On the Green

"Hiya."

Win turned to see who was speaking to him. He didn't recognize the voice.

It was late Friday afternoon. He had consulted again briefly with Laura—just a hunch—nothing he deemed important enough to involve June.

After convening with June at Elsie's apartment and being told about George's return of the watch, they had split for the day and he had driven to the range at the Crystal Springs Golf Course to hit balls and sort out in his head the various characters at the Plaza. Quite a few of them seemed to have been on intimate terms with the victim.

After hitting a bucketful, he felt better. Much better. And he stopped at the golf shop to chat with his pal, the pro, Paul.

The face addressing him looked familiar, but Win couldn't place the name. The golfer, a Payne Stewart look-alike in coordinated turtleneck, knickers, and jaunty cap, helped him out.

"We haven't officially met," he said, extending his hand. "I'm Bob Delaware. I live at the Plaza. Seen you around there plenty of times lately."

"Oh yeah," Win acknowledged. "My assistant told me about you."

"Yeah?" echoed Delaware. "So, how are you getting along? Got any leads yet?"

As if I'd tell you! Win thought to himself. Outwardly sociable, he replied, "Not yet."

"Well, never up, never in," Delaware said breezily, strolling to a bowl of golf balls for sale. "$1.50 each," read the sign.

"Here's for one, Paul," said Delaware, in a tone like master to servant, slapping a dollar bill on the counter and a couple of quarters. Win and Paul exchanged wry glances for Delaware had pocketed three balls for the price of one.

Delaware moved on to the electronic score-posting machine and activated its bells and whistles. Win, curious, sidled close by to see what the man had shot that day. A swift glance at Delaware's scorecard revealed eighty, but Win watched as Delaware nonchalantly posted an eighty-six.

Totally carefree, Delaware wheeled about and suggested to Win, "Wanta have a drink?"

"Sure," Win responded. He was curious to know more about this guy.

They adjourned to the bar. Each ordered a beer. Delaware took the lead in directing the conversation.

"So you're stymied, huh?" he said, with a crooked smile.

"Well, I wouldn't exactly say that," Win remonstrated.

"I know how it is to be handicapped," Delaware taunted. "All those rabbits. All those suckers. You've just gotta find the sweet spot."

"It's a little difficult with the situation here," Win said, deciding to play along with the man's goofy golf lingo. "Do you go by summer rules or winter rules?" he asked.

"Winter, always," blithely acknowledged Delaware. "And you?"

"Well, I take a Mulligan now and then," Win conceded. "I guess I feel entitled to, with the high greens fees they charge here."

"That's green," sneered Delaware.

"Pardon?" Win politely reacted.

"Green. Singular. Everybody says 'greens fee' "—Delaware said dramatically, rolling the "ssssss" on his tongue—"but it's green," he said positively and confidently, sounding the "n" like the toll of a gong.

Win listened, amused, as Delaware expounded on the explanation. The man was so goddamned determined!

"It's green," Delaware went on, like a fussy schoolmaster, "because you are paying to use the whole fucking course. In earliest days, golf was laid out in public parks. Get it? The local 'green.' "

Taking a swig and feeling superior, Delaware decided to further enlighten this stupid cop. "The men who look after the course are gree*n*keepers, not green*s*keepers. And here at the club we don't have a green*s* committee. It's a *green* committee, for God's sake."

"Oh," replied Win, pretending to be chastised.

"So, how's your equipment?" said Delaware, shifting gears.

"Well," Win started to answer...

"Do you hit it 'fat' or do you hit it 'thin'?" Delaware demanded to know.

"Gee," said Win. "I never thought about it."

"You'd better," scornfully rebutted Delaware, signaling the bartender for a refill.

"What's the loft on your driver?"

"Does it say?" said Win, feeling rather like a fool.

"Maybe yours doesn't. Mine does." Delaware said importantly. "Golfers need all the help they can get, you know. The higher the loft angle, the more backspin you can put on the ball," he said.

"Oh," said Win. "I didn't know that. I just play for fun."

"That so?" laughed Delaware, with a sort of sneer. "Pity. I was going to suggest we play sometime, but I always like to keep a bet going. I'd give you six strokes."

Recalling the inflated score he had seen Delaware post, Win let the offer pass, quaffing the last of his beer. *Hmmmm,* he thought. *Odd guy. He's even more of a golf nut than me.* Win got up to leave.

"Here's to luck on the dance floor!" said Delaware, saluting with his glass in a parting toast.

Excusing himself, Win went home to a TV dinner and a rented video and to work on his notes of the Johnson case. He was happy in anticipation of a more interesting evening to happen tomorrow. He had a date with June.

14
Phantom of the Night

It was late Friday night at the Plaza, and Millie, the mutt in 503, was restless. Something was wrong in the hallway outside the apartment, she sensed. She mewed like a kitten to get her owner's attention.

Groggy with sleep, Ruth Kenny stirred and leaned across the bed to speak to her pet. Its eyes were rolling in an attention-getting gesture, its head jerking toward the door. "Get up! Go look!" the dog was saying. But it was a vain effort. Ruth was too tired to get the message.

"Having a bad dream, sweetie?" she said. Affectionately, she soothed Millie's soft fuzzy head. "Settle down now. Good night, again!"

With a resigned sigh—after all, she'd *tried* to do her duty—Millie curled up, head on paws, and was instantly asleep.

Down the hall, in apartment 507, Stella Rankin woke, drummings of fright beating in her chest. Her heart began to pound. Someone was at her door! She could hear the rattling of a key probing for release of a tumble lock. She turned on the bedside light, and glanced at the clock. It was 3:00 A.M.

She hated nighttimes. Always had, since she'd been a little girl. The boogie men came then. They still did, she had admitted to a psychiatrist once. But this was no dream. The furtive, scuttling sounds were all too real.

She reached under the bed for a weapon she kept there—a hammer. She climbed out from between the sheets, and nearly tripped in the hem of her voluminous granny nightgown. She crept barefoot to the door and stood there, shaking and weak kneed.

She heard her name whispered. "Stel—-la!" It chilled her to the bone.

She tried holding her breath, exercising all her control not to scream. A gasp escaped her. Had she imagined it or had the door released a bit? Whoever was agitating it from the other side had managed to start the security chain rattling.

Her deadbolt was being tried now, and then her third lock, which sounded as if it were loosening.

Maybe whoever killed Elsie is after me? she thought, thoroughly terrified.

She took a firm grip on the hammer and stood stolidly, prepared for the worst, ready to defend herself.

Suddenly the rattlings ceased, as the person gave up trying to gain entry. She tiptoed to the peephole, and peered through. Although the hallway was brightly lit, her vision was distorted. What she saw came through like a crazy house of mirrors at an amusement park.

She fought her panic, and forced herself to look again. But all she saw was a shadowy, amorphous image moving rapidly away from her door, down the hall, toward the stairs. Was the head unusually large? Or was the person wearing some kind of hood? Something about him seemed familiar. For she had no doubt it was a "he."

Well, at least he's gone. Waves of relief swept over her. "Get hold of yourself," she scolded, climbing back into bed. It was probably just one of the new tenants, coming home late, getting off at the wrong floor, and mistaking his door for mine.

She slid between the sheets and burrowed down deep, pulling the covers, childlike, over her head. It was nothing to worry about, she told herself. Nothing. Still, she must remember to tell Laura about it in the morning.

Sleep returned to her, but disturbed, with distorted dreams. This was nothing new. Her dreams usually *were* weird. Jolting back to consciousness after particularly tortured dreams, the thought sometimes struck her that she might be on the verge of insanity.

In her unconsciousness now all was confusion. She dreamt fitfully of a chase. Of being chased. Or was it she who was chasing somebody? It was all going around and around in her mind. Elsie. The ambulance. The fire engine. The police cars. The flashing lights. The detective. His knock at her door, and the questions. She tossed and turned, but actually slept more than she realized. For suddenly she bolted awake with another start. Somebody was running down the hall!

The footfalls were heavy and clumsy. They hesitated at her door. Her heart began thumping. The sound of the footsteps passed. She flicked on the light and again looked at the clock. Two hours had passed. It was 5:30 A.M. Almost dawn.

A flash of reality hit her. "Oh, you fool!" Stella said to herself with a small relieved laugh. It's only the paper boy.

15
The Klatsch

Laura and five of the ladies had gathered in the lobby Saturday morning for their usual coffee klatsch. Yesterday, Laura had been distracted and short with them, claiming extra duties needing to be done. The ladies felt more welcome today. They chatted busily back and forth, but in agitated voices.

Three days had passed since the discovery of Elsie's body. Helen Emmons, of apartment 608, was particularly upset. "I just don't understand," she burbled, "why the police aren't any further along. They're just going to have to get more aggressive." She fluttered her hands as she spoke. It was one of her more irritating gestures. The spaniel, Pepper, sprawled at her feet, looked up and yawned.

"Well, of course they must be very careful," said Laura, defensively. She'd become fond of the detective and the lady cop. They were like family, being in the building so much.

Laura was their in-house informant, telling Win and June all newsy items that reached her ears. She didn't think she should tell the ladies this, however. Better let them just prattle on. She might learn something.

"No excuse!" barked Mary Hudson, agreeing with Helen. "They should use their wits more and look around and snoop!" A woman with hatchetlike features, she had once been a governess and still maintained a sharp, disciplinary attitude. Mary lived on the second floor and doted on Agatha Christie mysteries.

"I just don't know what this building is coming to," chimed in timid Dorothy Springer of 505. "This used to be such a nice place to live, but now, well, I don't know... I may have to move..." Her quivery voice trailed off nervously.

"Now, ladies," spoke up Laura, "don't worry. I'm sure everything will work out all right. Here, have a doughnut," she added, passing a plate around.

Laura's hostess gesture masked the frustration that she, too, felt. For an air of suspicion had permeated the Plaza. This peaceful, refined, safe, sociable building that she'd worked so hard to make into the most desirable address in Burlingame!

She was extremely particular whom she took in as tenants, careful to check references and all other screenings that the law allowed. Had this been for naught? For the Plaza now seemed to be holding its breath. Neighbor eyed neighbor furtively. It was as if each person wondered, "Were you the one who killed Elsie?"

Earlier that morning, Stella Rankin had told Laura of her frightening experience the night before. *A hooded phantom, indeed! I'd better not tell the ladies that,* Laura decided. *That would really freak them out! But,* she reminded herself, *I must remember to report it to Sergeant Winslow and Officer Jacobs. Who knows? It might be important.*

Oh, how Laura longed for the return of the good old days. Hopefully, life would be back to normal soon. But how could she convey this confidence to her ladies? All she could think of was to offer another cup of coffee.

Nobody was more eager than Helen Emmons to join in the game of sleuth. Helen craved excitement. Problem was, no one on her sixth floor seemed unusual to her. They were just a normal collection of ordinary people. Except, of course, for Mimi . . .

Come to think of it, odd sounds *did* come from her apartment. Next trip down the hall, she would dawdle by Mimi's door and listen more attentively.

Phyllis James, who lived on the first floor, next to the Chins, thought perhaps she had something to contribute. "I'm in and out all the time," she said. This was true. Phyllis seized each day as if it were her last.

A mild stroke years before had left her with a tremor. Her head continually bobbed up and down, making her look as if she agreed with everything said. Even her own words. Unlike some of her age group who pattered about in their robes until well past noon, Phyllis made herself get up at seven, dress, and hustle out to the lobby right after breakfast. Watching people come and go was her favorite pastime. "Nobody gets by me," she bragged. "And you know, I think I have a suspect. The big oaf who lives down my hall. You all know him. Mervin?" Her head bobbed in affirmative answer to herself.

"There's something odd about him," she declared.

Marguerite Gannett of the fourth floor piped up at that. She had a voice as strident as a bluejay, which she used effectively in her volunteer job for the Peninsula Blood Bank, phoning around for reluctant donors. She never took no for an answer. And now she had her own neighbor fingered. "That slick Mr. Levin on *my* floor is a real sly fellow," she said.

"Ladies, ladies!" Laura protested. "Everybody's innocent until proven guilty!" She meant to be funny. But nobody laughed.

Near noon, the ladies had exhausted their gossip, and Laura was wearying of them. Longing for them to be gone, she saw an opportunity to break up the group. "Oh, look! The mail's here!" she announced. "Excuse me, ladies," she added, seeing a legitimate reason to escape. Win and June were about to enter the building. She went forth to greet them, eager to tell them of Stella's weird story of the night before.

"Hi, Don!" the ladies chorused, rising en masse to greet the mailman. Like a flock of squawking seagulls, they swooped around his work area.

"Now, ladies, give me room," he ordered, shooing them away. Don was in a snit, for he had many magazines to sort this day.

Mary Hudson watched as he tossed three thick issues into the W bin. She was always interested to learn who subscribed to what. She often "borrowed" other people's magazines when nobody was looking. Mary had done this numerous times with Elsie Johnson's subscriptions, but it didn't seem right to invade the J box anymore.

"Bob *Woods?*" she read over Don's shoulder, puzzled. "I thought I knew everyone in the building. Don't believe I know him."

"You do, too," Don snorted. "That's the name Mr. Delaware writes under. He gets a lot of his mail like that."

"*Two* names? How conceited of him," Mary snorted. "Oh, hello!" she said in her next breath.

The detective and policewoman had just passed by. They smiled cordially and continued to the elevator, looking at each other meaningfully as the doors closed behind them.

16
The Strange Ones

Since they were alone in the elevator, June said tentatively, "Win?" After all, who was she to make a suggestion? *He* was the boss. But they were making a deplorable lack of progress. Or so it seemed to her quick, impulsive nature. What did she have to lose by speaking up? Nothing, she decided, except being taken off the assignment. Did she want to risk that? Yes! Nothing ventured, nothing gained, as her mother liked to say. She cleared her throat, summoning up confidence to continue.

"Yes?" prompted Win. He looked at her, smiled, and gave her his full attention. This was easy to do. More and more, he was pleased by her. Not only was she great to look at, but she said what she thought. No games, no airs. No reluctance to speak her mind. And what she had to say was always to the point. She was a fine balance, he felt, for his careful, slow, inclined-to-be-plodding ways.

"Do you think it means anything that Delaware goes by another name?" she asked him.

"Could be," he said, vaguely. "But first things first. Let's see what Mr. Levin has to say for himself."

She nodded, punching 4.

Leon Levin was damned if he'd let the police team know he was alarmed to find them knocking at his door.

"Good morning," Win said pleasantly to him.

"Good day to you, sir," Levin answered, formally. He spoke in a clipped and precise English patterned after his hero, the legendary film actor David Niven.

He frowned to see that they were accompanied by that damn grinning police dog. Levin despised dogs.

When a dog ventured too close to him, as sometimes happened when the elevator was crowded, he had a game he liked to play. He would twitch his feet as if he were about to do a tap dance. People would smile indulgently, thinking him a harmless old fool, but the dogs knew better. The gesture was a warning that he would happily kick them if he had a chance to do so. He had never actually done it and probably never would, for the mock tap dance was sufficient. The dogs always kept their distance from him. Naturally, Levin controlled himself, facing the large dog, Chief. He wasn't about to attract undue attention to himself.

"May we come in?" he was being asked.

"Of course," he replied, in his most civil tone. Why not? He had nothing to hide.

For the second time, their eyes roved around his apartment. Win noticed with a pang of interest that where there'd been one, there were now two old golf club/canes standing in the corner.

June was drawn to a black hooded cape hanging from a peg in the hallway. It was what Levin ceremoniously wore to the opening of the San Francisco Opera every year. Oh-oh, Levin thought, recalling his foolishness of the night before.

Aloud he said, in a peevish tone, "I say, what *are* you looking for?"

"Did you wear this cape last night?" Win asked.

"I don't believe so. No, of course I didn't."

"Are you sure, Mr. Levin?" pressed June. "We have a witness who says there was a hooded figure at her door around 3:00 A.M. It frightened her. Was it you?"

"Oh, bother," Levin conceded, with an annoyed flutter of his wrist. "I was just having a little fun."

"At three o'clock in the morning, scaring a woman half to death?" Win angrily reacted.

"Well, I didn't do any harm. And I wouldn't have," Levin answered defensively. "I couldn't sleep, you see," he explained. "This building has gotten so blasted grim lately. I just thought I'd liven things up a bit. Miss Rankin never says boo. I thought I could get a rise out of her. Might draw her out of her shell. You know, she could be quite attractive, if she tried."

"Don't do it again," the sergeant ordered. "That's harassment, you know."

"No, I don't suppose I will," Levin answered, sarcastically.

"By the way, Mr. Levin," June added. "Do you drink?"

"A nip from time to time," Levin acknowledged.

"Do you like Scotch?" Win asked.

"Can't stand the stuff," Levin sniffed. "I'm a champagne man, myself."

"One more thing, Mr. Levin," said Win. "Your walking sticks . . . these golf clubs . . . did they come from Mrs. Johnson?"

"As a matter of fact, they did," Levin allowed, huffily.

"Were they a gift or did you help yourself to them?"

"Really, Officer!" Levin snapped, eyes blazing. "How very insulting! Of course they were gifts! She would tell you herself if she were here!" His eyes welled with tears of emotion, and satisfied that he was telling the truth, Win and June departed.

Stella Rankin, who lived in apartment 507, could have walked out of a Charles Addams cartoon. Skinny, gaunt, pale, with mousey gray hair, she had a strange way of dressing. She favored ankle-length black skirts, long-sleeved shirts buttoned tight at the neck, bobby socks, and clumpy white Reeboks.

According to the coffee klatsch, Stella's odd ways were the result of having experimented with drugs many years ago while a student at the University of California at Berkeley.

Now in her fifties, she had a perpetual droop to her mouth. Whenever she spoke, it was to complain. The weather, the building, a tenant, the town. Nothing pleased her.

She had a sneaky way of moving. More than once, a tenant stepping into an apparently empty elevator would jump with alarm, finding Stella already inside, standing in the corner quiet as a mouse.

Rumor had it that she was an artist, but nobody knew if this was true, for no one had been invited inside her apartment. Not even Win, with his official police questions.

"My privacy is very important to me," she had explained.

Now he was at her door again. This time with the policewoman and the big black dog.

She opened the door a crack, and patiently waited, with a disconcerting stare, for what they had to say. They didn't ask to come in.

"We just wanted to tell you, ma'am," Win said, "that the prowler last night *was* your neighbor, Mr. Levin. I believe that's what you suspected, according to what Mrs. Fiedler told us?"

Stella nodded. In the clear light of morning, she had made the connection between the "unusually large head" she'd glimpsed through the peephole and the hooded cape she'd seen Leon flaunt on his seasonal opera sprees.

"He meant no harm," Win told her. "He considered it a prank. A *very* stupid prank, he agrees.

"We had a talk with him," Win added. "It won't happen again. Do you want to press charges?"

"No. It's all right," Stella answered, in her strange, almost whispering voice. "Thank you for telling me."

It was the first pleasant thing she'd said in years.

There being no reason to connect her with the death of Elsie, they left. Stella slipped back inside her apartment, to resume her secret project.

17
A Walk around the Block

"So what do we do now?" Jane asked Win, upon leaving Stella's.

"We need some fresh air," he said. "Let's take a walk around the block."

They strode briskly down Chapin, the dog Chief gliding along beside them. They passed Burlingame Garden Center and automatically glanced to the right to admire the glorious bursts of floral color. They strolled on. Win reached in his jacket pocket for his notebook.

"So what do we know about Elsie?" he mused, thumbing the pages. "Besides her being bossy, domineering, and intrusive?"

"She meant well," June ventured.

"That may be, but she sure rubbed somebody the wrong way. Did she have any family?"

"Negative. I checked that out the first day. She was an only child. No children of her own. No sisters, no brothers, no cousins, no nothing. Her husband died twenty years ago. He was a stockbroker. A good one too. He left her very well off, judging by the Shearson Lehman statements and the checkbook that I found in one of her drawers."

Win's head snapped alert. "Did it look as if she was unusually wealthy?"

"Lord, yes," June answered.

"I've never heard of anyone keeping fifty thousand dollars in a checking account that paid practically no interest. And," she added, "the market value of her investments was in seven figures. Considering she lived alone, had no debts and no dependents, yeah, I'd say Elsie was *very* wealthy. But you know what's strange? All her financial papers were more or less in plain sight. But I never saw a will."

"Ah," responded Win, softly, "now who might have been after that money?"

They rounded the corner onto Primrose, heads bent toward each other in talk.

On her lunch hour, Ruth Kenny was walking Millie and Angus. Only it was more like a trot. Devoted as she was to Nancy Webb, there were times when she regretted the extra noontime chore of looking after Angus. She didn't usually do it on weekends, but Nancy had asked if she would, just this once.

And today, the Scottie seemed obsessed to sprint along with a surge of energy as other dogs in the building came into sight. Ironically, her own passive Millie seemed to be in cahoots with Angus, dashing beside him with a panting grin.

Inevitably, Ruth would get their leashes entangled with one of the other dogs. She tried to make a joke of it. "Dogs will be dogs, won't they!" she had laughed to Mrs. Emmons, who made a tolerably pleasant reply. But two of the other owners, Bob Delaware and Mr. Chin, seemed distinctly annoyed when she tried the same line on them.

And what was the matter with Bob's poodle, Gigi? Usually she was the most genial of dogs, her pompom of a tail a spinning sign of happiness. But today she'd seemed forlorn, head hung low, tail drooping.

Ah, well, Ruth didn't have time to think about it. Her lunch hour was going by all too fast. Her canine pals were ruling the day. She resented it. But then she would laugh helplessly at the ridiculous situation, noticing how much her charges were enjoying themselves.

What a cocky little fellow that Angus was. So inquisitive and bossy. Just like a man. She laughed again and then, remembering the lateness of the time, jerked sharply on their leashes. "Come on, kids, I've got to get back to work," she said, hurrying them home and leaving them.

About 3:00 P.M., Leon Levin, in suit, vest, and golf stick/cane, was strutting along Primrose Avenue, bound for his favorite place, the Burlingame Library. In hot pursuit was the dachshund Hans, straining at his leash to the consternation of his master, George, who was on his midafternoon coffee break.

The three had just descended in the elevator together. Leon had been his usual aloof, twitchy-footed self. Not wanting to chance getting kicked, Hans had sidled behind his master. George noticed, but wanting no trouble with his peculiar neighbor, had kept silent, too.

"Hey, slow down!" George puffed ineffectually. Hans's short stumpy legs pumped furiously at propelling his fat sausage of a body as fast as possible down the street. Although George had no intention of going into the library, he found himself yanked up the steps and dragged inside as Hans tracked his quarry.

Ruth Kenny, on duty at the counter, held up a warning hand. "Sorry, George," she reminded him. "You know the rules. No dogs allowed."

"Long as I'm here, I might as well take out a book," George said. He took Hans outside, tied him to a railing, and went back in. He walked directly to his favorite section, center aisle, top shelf, last row down on the left. To his most favorite author. He knew the shelf practically by heart. Ah! The author's latest was there! He reached for it eagerly and strode to the checkout counter.

Leon Levin was already there, checking out *his* book. George strained to see what it was. His open honest face registered surprise. Leon, in turn, looked to see George's choice. His eyes twinkled. His mouth smirked. He couldn't control himself. He laughed out loud.

"Quiet, please!" Ruth said, automatically, thinking to herself as she stamped both men's books. "Boy, you never know!"

George ambled out with the latest Stephen King horror. Leon, with the newest mushy romance by Danielle Steel.

Mr. Chin was in a playful frame of mind. "When one's life is bounded by four main streets, one must widen the eyes," he told his little family in a joking Confucious Knows imitation, gathering them and the dog Ming for a walk around the block.

He chose, this day, the southern route—a turn to the right off Chapin onto Primrose, thence through the heart of town, along busy Burlingame Avenue, and home.

Although he considered himself a cosmopolite, Mr. Chin never ceased to be amazed at the entertaining spectacle of everyday life in this town. Why, it was better than going to the movies. Nearly all the people they passed wore dark glasses, making it seem like a town for blind persons. And certainly a town with a split personality.

Burlingame is both reminiscent of an English village with its pitching, gray slate roofs and red brick chimneys and loyal to its Spanish heritage, with some buildings stuccoed in white with roofs of red tile. At the foot of

Burlingame Avenue is the railroad station, a bilious mustard-colored mission-revival design, dating to 1894. It was, Mr. Chin informed his family, financed by the Burlingame Country Club (now heavily into golf, but not then) to bring participants and spectators down from San Francisco for their polo games and coyote hunts.

"Why they call it Burlingame?" Mrs. Chin asked as they strolled along.

Mr. Chin was pleased to enlighten her. "In 1866, when Abraham Lincoln was president . . ." he began.

Mrs. Chin nodded wisely.

" . . . Mr. Anson Burlingame was the U.S. ambassador to China. He passed through here on his way to the Orient and bought a thousand acres of land."

"Hee hee," Mrs. Chin giggled, at the Chinese connection. "Did he live here?"

"No, never. It was just an investment. But it got other people interested in the area, and so it became a town. They honored him by naming it Burlingame."

"He must have been pleased," Mrs. Chin ventured bravely. Rarely did she voice an opinion to her husband.

"He never knew," Mr. Chin informed her. "He died in Russia in 1870."

"Oh," Mrs. Chin answered. What more was there to say?

The Chin family clung dutifully to each other's hands as they strolled along, observing the colorful local life. The fluffy Shih-Tzu fussily led the way.

Many small shops in the town had cute catchy names. Mrs. Chin, who was into needlework, brought the group to a halt to peer into the Status Thimble. The little daughter eyed the grown-up goodies in the window of the seductive bath shop, Bare Necessities. They all slowed to peer through the bars of the below-the-street window of the

Shear Ecstasy haircutting salon. They passed the law office with its name in blinking lights on a marquee, as at a movie theater. And such an ironic name—Juris Dumpis!

They paused before All That Glitters, the gaudy costume jewelry boutique. This was one of their favorite stops, for the displays were so unusual. Featured today was the American flag in rhinestones and fake turquoise and diamonds. The red-white-and-blue had been fashioned into G-strings, pointy bras, buckles, belts, earrings, pins, and dangling necklaces meant to swing patriotically to and fro between a woman's breasts. Clucking at the audacity, the family passed on. They slowed their steps to peer over the Dutch door of the antique shop, Whistling Swan. What was "antique" to Americans was ridiculously modern to Mrs. Chin, so these shops, too, were good for a chuckle.

The Bits and Pieces china and glassware shop caught their interest next. Because the smooth cement sidewalks, flecked with shimmering mica, felt hotly uncomfortable to his tender pads, Ming hustled the family on, past the shoe repair shop, past the smoke shop, onto the classier part of Burlingame Avenue where the walkway was of aggregate, tiny little pebbles set in cement and far easier for his dog feet to take.

They crossed the avenue and broke ranks for a visit to the Baskin Robbins ice cream store, where all lapped a cone, dog included. After the treat, aware of the very proper picture they presented, Mr. Chin detoured his flock past Burger King and its loitering, faintly threatening, boisterous teenage gangs and onto the red-bricked crossway.

They were about to examine the latest classic fashions in the windows of the genteel Texas-based store, Malouf, when a disturbance caught their attention. Being at eye-level with the sidewalk, Ming noticed it first. A familiar shoe was suddenly thrust into his view. It was followed by a second shoe, its mate. Two unsteady legs, clad in jeans, rose from them.

Craning his neck, Ming recognized their big, burly neighbor, Merv, who lived down the hall at the Plaza. Drunk and belligerent, Merv had just been thrown out of the Bit of England Pub.

"I'll get you for this!" he yelled, slobberingly, fists weakly upraised, at the bartender who hollered back, "Go home and sleep it off, Merv! You're lucky I don't call the cops!"

As Merv lurched on the sidewalk, seeking his balance and some semblance of dignity, he half-recognized his shocked neighbors. "Oh, pardon me, little doggy," he slurred, staggering on his feet.

Embarrassed by their neighbor, and for themselves by having witnessed him in such a condition, the Chin family scuttled home.

18
The Note

"So, now what?" June asked Win, upon their return to the Plaza.

He flipped through his notebook and tapped a page he had filled with exclamation marks. "I want to ask Laura something. Come on," he said cryptically. They strolled down the hall to her office.

"What can you tell us about Miss Masterson?" Win asked Laura.

Laura's eyebrows flew up, startled. "Miss Masterson? Oh, I never think of her by that name. You mean *Mimi!* She's a darling! Always bringing me candy or flowers. Surely you don't suspect *her?*"

"Ma'am?" Win politely prodded.

"Well," Laura began reluctantly, "she's lived here a long time. Since way before I came. According to my records, her name was different then. I guess she was married. I've never asked. She pays her rent on time. Seems to have plenty of friends. I honestly don't know much more about her."

"Was she on good terms with Elsie?" June asked.

Laura shifted in her seat. "From what I could see, I wouldn't exactly say friendly, but they certainly knew who each other was.

"Everybody does here at the Plaza."

Behind them, the door from the street opened. Don, the mailman, entered and started fussing around the mailboxes in the alcove behind the office.

"You're awfully early today, aren't you?" called out Laura.

"I had an extra load," he hollered back. "Thought I'd get rid of it."

Leaving his post for a moment, he sauntered over and stood in the office doorway. "Did I hear you asking about Miss Masterson?" he asked.

The three others looked up, expectantly.

"Have you something to tell us?" Win prompted.

"Well, I don't know if this means anything or not," Don began. He hesitated, realizing he was about to commit a cardinal sin—something a postman is not supposed to do. Don loved to read other people's mail.

"Yes?" Win urged.

Don sighed. He'd gone too far to stop now. He continued. "Miss Masterson used to get a lot of little notes in her box from Mrs. Johnson. They were just folded slips of paper, you know? No envelopes. No seals. Just pieces of paper shoved through the slot.

"I'd find them when I opened up the boxes to put the mail in and of course I couldn't help but notice who they were from."

"Of course," June nodded, encouragingly.

Seeing he had the detective and the policewoman's attention, he added importantly, "The notes were all along the same line . . . don't do this, don't do that. Kind of like a mother would talk to a daughter, you know?

"Another thing. Miss Masterson gets an awful lot of mail. Stuff marked 'Personal'. A lot of forwardings from a post office box in San Francisco."

"You don't say!" Win reacted. "Well, thanks for telling us this."

With a carefree shrug, Don wheeled about and resumed his sorting. Win caught June's eye with a "Let's go" expression. "Thanks for your time," he said to Laura. "We'll get out of your hair now."

Chief, who'd been sitting by Laura's desk, sprang to his feet, smartly. Wordlessly, they moved as a team to the elevator, to the third floor, and Elsie's apartment. By this time, they had their own key.

"What are we looking for?" June asked, once they were inside 308.

"A diary or address book would be my guess. Something to tie the victim in with Mimi," Win explained.

They scattered, opening drawers of Elsie's many little tables, rummaging about.

"Maybe this!" June called from the bedroom. She emerged, waving an address book.

"Woof!" barked Chief at the excitement in her voice.

Win was at her side in an instant. "What have you got?" he asked.

"Bonanza!" she said, triumphantly, having flipped to the Ms and discovered a note tucked between the pages.

Together they read it, their eyes glinting at this first real break in the case. In a large, looping feminine sprawl, the note read, "I'm getting sick and tired of your stares and your silly notes. Stay out of my life. I'm warning you, I'll take action if you don't." It was neither dated nor signed.

"Mimi's writing?" queried June.

"I betcha," Win replied. "Let's see if Laura can identify it."

They returned to the office. Showing Laura the handwriting, June was careful to hold the note so that only the word "stares" showed. That had enough letters to identify with the Masterson signature Laura knew so well from the monthly rent checks.

"Yes, Mimi wrote this," Laura confirmed.

"Let's go talk with her," Win said to June.

They rode upstairs again, this time to 605.

19
Mimi

Of all the people who lived at the Plaza, Mimi Masterson was the most noticeable. She would have stood out in any crowd, with her flaming red hair.

She hadn't always been a redhead. Nor had she always been "Mimi." Ten years before, when she'd moved into the Plaza, she was just plain Mary Margaret Hogan, twenty-two, dowdy brunette, bookish, timid, and wife of Joe Hogan, an aggressive fellow who worked as a sales rep for a computer company.

Joe took a perverse pleasure in confusing his shy little wife. He would belittle and downgrade her one day and overwhelm her with sweet loving the next. He was her first beau, the only young man she had ever known. Whatever he wanted to do, she did. No questions. No resistance. Certainly no back talk.

Her mother, a notorious nag, had brought her up to believe that "men know best," even though her husband, Mary Margaret's father, had abandoned the family when the child was only three. From the age of eighteen, Mary Margaret had been pressured by her mother to find a man and get married. She had been passably pretty at twenty, and vivacious enough to be noticed by Hogan.

On their honeymoon he had insisted on taking her on a seven-day horseback pack trip through the High Sierras.

Knowing nothing of horses and frightened of them, she was terrified the whole time, which amused Hogan mightily. Hating herself for being so cowardly, she managed to struggle through the horrible wedding trip . . . saddle sores, knee burns, and all.

They moved to Burlingame, so that Joe could be closer to his extensive territory—San Mateo to San Jose. And upon settling into the Park Plaza Apartments, Mary Margaret haunted the Burlingame Public Library for every conceivable book on horses. The pack trip had been such a miserable experience she was obsessed with the determination to learn all she could about horses, to conquer her fear.

Mary Margaret threw her energies into the world of horses. She bought a mare on time payments, stabling it at a boarding ranch in Woodside. She invested in riding lessons, began entering horse shows, and became adept at the exacting demands of dressage. When she finally felt she had conquered her fear of horses, she threw it all away. Sold the horse. Disposed of her riding gear.

She rid herself of Hogan, too. That was easy. He had a wandering eye, anyway, and was only too happy to call the short marriage quits and to pay her a reasonable alimony. It was worth it to him to have his freedom back.

She dropped the name Hogan. Took back her maiden name, Masterson. Had her hair colored. And instead of dull, boring Mary Margaret, she henceforth called herself "Mimi." She even had her checks printed that way.

Next, she turned to dominating men. Began bringing them home for sex. Not for money; she was no whore. She did it just for the fun of it. And to make men her puppets. She met them everywhere: "chance meetings" while browsing the video racks at the Sneak Preview store, waiting in line at Burger King, pumping gas at the Chevron station. Behind closed doors, Mimi was a hoyden, a vixen—insatiable.

She had arranged her apartment to be a virtual den of sin, a laughable spoof of bawdy houses as remembered from her most favorite movies. It was designed for incredible entertainment. As Win had found out, an enormous daybed was the chief piece of furniture in the living room.

The bedroom was a virtual garden of Eden, with luxuriant ferns hanging on hooks from the ceiling. A large TV faced her big round bed. She kept her compact disc player in the bedroom, too. It had superb sound. The speakers, as set up by not-always-shy George Schmidt of the fourth floor, made even the most innocuous song sound like a rapturous symphony.

Mimi relished her wild way of life. The minute she came home, she would strip off her clothes and joyfully waltz around naked, demanding that her male visitors do likewise. Mimi's was the only apartment in the building where the drapes were always drawn.

Recently, ecstatic cries of "Ooooooh, Mimi!" were heard out in the "sound-proof" corridor. The happy yells sent the spaniel, Pepper, who lived down the hall, into spasms of howling as Mimi's man of the moment received full enjoyment.

Mimi's latest kick was joining a "Swingles Club," featuring a computerized dating service. She also ran suggestive ads in the Personals column of *Focus* magazine, the monthly publication of KQED, San Francisco's public broadcasting station. These were P.O. Box ads, that she would either answer or not, depending on her mood when she read the replies.

Mimi would meet her frequent dates in the lobby of the Plaza, and if they seemed OK and not too kinky, she would bring them upstairs to apartment 605.

All this hectic activity, and her ups and down in the elevator with so many different men, had been noticed with great interest, concern, and alarm by Elsie Johnson of 308. Elsie saw in Mimi the daughter she had never had. She had been determined to halt this scandalous behavior.

Elsie would go out of her way to encounter Mimi, on the street, in a store, in the lobby of the Plaza. She would trail Mimi into the elevator, and if they were alone, which Elsie would make sure to happen, the older woman would try to draw the younger one into conversation and then chide and scold her.

Lately, Elsie had taken to leaving notes at Mimi's door. They were "You must be careful, you are ruining your life" kind of notes, that Elsie would slip beneath the doorsill. While she was at it, she would listen for sounds of sex from inside.

Mimi had tried shrugging off Elsie's meddlings. But one day she had had enough and had written the older woman a strong note of her own. This was the note with a threatening tone that June had found in Elsie's address book.

Elsie had no intention of dropping her salvation mission. And so she had answered the note by inviting Mimi in for cocktails and what she hoped would be a decisive meeting. Mimi had accepted, with the plan to insist once and for all that Elsie get out of her life.

It didn't work that way. Elsie, as always, had the upper hand. When she said to Mimi, "You should see a psychiatrist, dear. I can help if it's a matter of money..." Mimi grew hot with anger. She had leapt to her feet, spilling her drink, and stormed out of apartment 308, banging the door behind her. "You meddlesome old fool!" she had shrieked. "I could kill you!"

"So did you?" demanded Win, perched uneasily on the edge of the come-hither bed, the only place to sit in her living room.

"Of course not," retorted Mimi, who had told him and June only the part of her story that related to the note.

"Where were you last Monday night, Miss Masterson?" Win asked.

"Right here," she answered, nonchalantly.

"Can you prove that?" he pressed.

"I sure can," she replied. "I had a friend here with me from four o'clock that afternoon until 8:00 A.M. Tuesday morning. We never left this apartment.

"And I don't mind telling you one other thing," she added. "Elsie was a terrible pest. I can't say I'm sorry she's dead."

Some tough cookie, Win thought to himself. Only the slightest lift of a shaggy eyebrow betrayed his feelings.

He rose to leave. June and Chief followed. Mimi walked them to the door, perfunctorily offering a handshake to each. They were surprised by the strength of her grip. Hands strong enough to choke with? Perhaps.

20
Getting to Know You

Win paused at the picket gate of 1010 Walnut Street, officially in Burlingame but on the borderline with the haughty community of Hillsborough. He smiled at what he saw.

June's home was much as he had imagined it would be. Neat and trim, one-story, ranch style, stained a natural redwood color. It had large generous windows set off by white trim, allowing lots of fresh air and light. A small, close-cropped lawn swept from the sidewalk to just before the house, where a generous border of impatiens took over, gayly blooming in reds, pinks, and orange.

After three days of working as a team, he and June had felt increasingly relaxed with each other. It was a fine working relationship with a possibility of growing into something more personal. June had invited him for dinner this Saturday evening. Pleased and flattered, he had accepted.

He opened the gate, and closed it behind him. He walked quickly and eagerly to the door. There was no need to know. She'd been watching for him and stood in the doorway in welcome. The dog, Chief, was at her side, big broom of a tail waving madly.

"Hi! I'm glad you could come!" she said, reaching out and shaking his hand. She'd have preferred to give him a hug, but better not—yet—she thought.

They stood for an instant, each sizing the other up, pleased with each other's looks off duty. June looked adorable, her curly blond hair bobbing free around her shoulders, her lithe body clothed in pink slacks, floral shirt, and open-toed sandals.

Win was similarly casual, tan pants, pale blue, short-sleeved button-down shirt, no tie, loafers. He looked as if he didn't have a care in the world. A stranger meeting him would never have guessed his profession to be detective, a person often, if not usually, seeing the seamy side of life.

He followed her inside. "Nice house!" he exclaimed.

"Thanks! It's really Mother's. She moved to Oakmont after Dad died, but since the house was all paid for she decided to keep it. And I'm the lucky one who gets to be caretaker. No rent, either!" she grinned.

"You *are* lucky," he agreed, thinking ruefully of his ever-escalating rent at the nondescript Broadway Apartments.

Playfully, Chief nuzzled his elbow. The dog loped ahead of them to the kitchen, picked up his food dish, and deposited it at Win's feet.

"That seems to be a hint," Win remarked, amused.

"Yuh. I'll feed him. Why don't you mix us a drink? Vodka-tonic for me. But there's scotch and bourbon."

He busied himself. *Interesting,* she thought, stealing a peek as she opened the refrigerator, *how natural he seems here in my house. He is sort of cute. Maybe a little old for me . . . maybe not.*

"Ah," he exclaimed, totally unaware of her calculating glances and sniffing appreciatively at the delicious aroma wafting from the large covered skillet on the stove. "What are we having?"

"Coq au vin. I hope you like it. I haven't made it for ages." (Too true, she mused, recalling the last time—a disastrous supper party when her guest of honor had stomped out before dinner in a silly jealous huff.)

"Smells great," Win assured her. "Quite a change from my usual spaghetti and meat balls!"

While Chief bolted his Alpo and kibble, they moved into the living room, settling side by side on the couch. On the table was an album of snapshots. Curious, he picked it up and idly began flipping through it.

"Lovely woman. Your mother?"

June nodded.

He paused at another photo. It was June on a beach, looking up fondly and holding hands with an attractive man.

"Boyfriend?"

"Father!" she laughed.

"That was five years ago, when he was still feeling good," she explained. "Maybe you knew him? He was in Investigations too."

"I wish I had known him," said Win softly. "I've only been with the department here four years, you know. I've sure heard about him, though. He must have been a hell of a guy."

"He sure was," she said, wistfully.

Win flipped to another page.

"Boyfriend?" he asked again.

"Used to be!" she laughed. *Enough of this beating-around-the-bush,* she thought. "How about you?" she asked. "Do you have a girl?"

"Nope," he answered, adding, in case she was interested, "I *have* been married, though."

"Oh?" (She knew that already, having looked him up in the department's personnel file. But she feigned surprise.)

"It was a long time ago," he said. "I was about your age."

She made a face, not liking his remark alluding to the fourteen-year spread in their ages. Catching his goof, he hastily added, "My wife and I were only together three years."

"Divorced?"

"No, she died."

"Oh, I'm sorry," June said, instinctively touching his hand.

"Don't be," he reacted. "It was a blessing, really. She had an inoperable cancer. It went very quickly. We were lucky. She really didn't suffer at all."

Eager to change the subject, he blurted out the quickest thing that popped to mind. Baseball. The season had just begun. "So, who's your favorite league this year?"

Relieved to be off the subject of his wife, but secretly pleased to learn he didn't have a girl, June responded "American, I guess. I'm a Giants' fan." She wasn't really versed on baseball, but made a stab at faking it.

"Let's hope they have a winning team this time," Win answered. With him, too, it was a half-hearted remark. He wasn't all that crazy about baseball, either.

It had been a long time since he had made small talk with a date. Gad, he was out of practice! He hoped he wasn't boring this darling girl. Desperately, he reached for another conversational gambit. "Do you like golf at all?"

"Now there's a dull sport," June responded. "All those people with big bellies riding around in dodge 'em cars, jumping out to hit a little ball, and riding on again. Sure looks dumb to me."

Win felt himself bristle, golf being his favorite pastime. But he sure didn't want to pick an argument at this early stage in their relationship.

"Golf *does* look hectic from the outside," he agreed. "But when you're on the course and involved in your own game problems, it's not that way at all. Besides, purists like me walk! And that's a whole different game. You'd be surprised how intriguing golf is once you get into it. It's got a great history."

"A good walk spoiled!" she countered, teasingly.

"Funny you should say that. I have a book by that name," Win answered.

"I bet you think of golf as beginning in Scotland," he said.

She stared at him blankly.

"Well, the Chinese say they invented it. So do the Japanese. So do the Dutch."

Oh-oh, she thought. *I hope this isn't going to be a boring evening.*

He droned on, mistaking her silence for interest. "Originally, sticks and stones were used. As more people became hooked on the game, they demanded better equipment. Clubs were changed from wood to metal and balls from clumpy, carved wooden things to softer and even stranger materials."

Finally noticing her eyes glazing with uninterest, he hastily changed the subject. "But I know what you mean," he concluded. "Golf *does* take too long for most of us working stiffs. Especially if you can only play weekends. That's why I settle for running."

"Oh, really?" she sparkled. "I run, too."

She smiled, thinking of her favorite recreational area—a six-mile-long track for bikers and hikers that winds along the banks of the Crystal Springs Reservoir. Wandering below the coastal mountains leading to Half Moon Bay and the Pacific Ocean, it has tiny brooks and trickling streams and hills dotted with wildflowers and Scotch broom. Spanish moss drips from the trees, and redtail hawks circle overhead. To June it was incredibly beautiful. She had often wondered if the famous hills and lakes scenery of Ireland could be any grander.

She came out of her dream world, naming the place. "I run on the Sawyer Camp Trail."

"You're kidding!" Win exclaimed, delightedly. "That's where I go. Every Sunday morning. And you?"

"Saturdays," she answered. "Usually Saturdays, that is," she added, getting in a jibe for the extra hours he'd had her put in on the case the day before. "I go real early. Like seven."

"Seven's not too early for me," he picked up. "You can always get a parking space then. Say, why don't we run together some weekend? We could flip a coin as to who changes their day."

"Sounds great! Let's do it," she responded. Grabbing the moment, she added, "How about tomorrow?"

"You're on!" he said.

They sipped their drinks, chattering away at random. Chief stretched contentedly at their feet. They talked about the trail. "Did you know the San Andreas Fault crosses it?" he mentioned. A major weakness in the crust of the California earth, one of eight faults that slash like a dagger through the state, the San Andreas Fault causes occasional earthquakes when the land slides in opposite directions and rockspurs interlock within it.

"Really?" she responded. "I wonder what it would feel like to be running there when an earthquake happened?"

"I hope we never find out!" he chuckled.

"I bet you don't know who the Sawyer Camp Trail was named for," she teased.

"You got me," he said.

"Leander Sawyer," she informed him with a playful primness. "He was one of the early settlers who came out here after the Civil War. He ran a cattle ranch where the trail is now, and he also trained performing horses for traveling circuses. He ran an inn, too. Isn't that interesting?"

Win resisted the impulse to pat her on the shoulder like a smart little schoolgirl. Instead he said simply, "It is." And to his surprise, he meant it. "Guess I'm not as blasé as I thought I was," he said to himself.

Finally she asked, "Hungry?"

Oh, adorable girl, if you only knew, he thought, aching to hold and kiss her. Restraining himself, he merely answered, "You bet."

As if reading his true mind, she coyly leapt to her feet. So did Chief, although it took him a moment longer to untangle his long legs.

"Come!" she smiled, pulling Win from the sofa. "You can do the honors."

He followed her to the kitchen where, with a flourish, and a dramatic "Ta-Dum!" she removed the cover of the skillet from the simmering feast.

She produced a quarter of a cup of brandy and handed him a match. He struck it, and together they jumped back a step and laughed at the fun of the flames leaping—Pow!—from the succulent meal.

They ate by candlelight in the cozy dining room. Beneath the table, Chief lay dozing. Soft rock music played from the radio in the other room.

"I always liked that tune," Win commented. "Can't think of its name, though."

June smiled, mischievously. "After the Loving," she informed him.

"No wonder I like it!" he laughed.

Both had hearty appetites, and went back for seconds. Soon emptied was the bottle of wine, a smooth and expensive Pinot Noir from the Gundlach Bundschu winery in the

Sonoma Valley, which June had splurged on for this special occasion. Vanilla ice cream topped with hot fudge sauce brought dinner to a close. The candles were flickering low as they finished their demitasses.

Hand in hand, they retired to the living room.

"That was delicious," he said.

"It was, wasn't it!" she smiled.

She plumped the pillows on the sofa, and they settled down again. He wanted to tell her how much it meant to him to be here at her invitation, getting to know her better.

I'd better not, he thought. *It might sound presumptive. Besides, why would she be interested in an old fart like me?*

Instead, he said, "Do you mind if we talk about the case?"

"Of course not," she answered, wondering why it had taken him so long. After all, it was the uppermost thing on their minds. Well, almost uppermost . . . "I thought you'd want to," she said, encouragingly.

"It bothers me," he said, "that we don't seem to be getting anywhere."

Inwardly she laughed, for it was what she had been thinking so many times in the past few days. Earnestly, she answered, "Oh, but we are." Her brown eyes danced with double meaning.

Instantly, she regretted her flip remark, for Win, she thought, looked alarmed. *Cool it!* she said to herself. *You don't want to scare him off.* Quickly she added, "Have you noticed how the dogs at the building seem to be getting into the act?"

"You know, I have!" he answered. "I thought I was imagining it at first. A couple of days ago, the spaniel grabbed my pants cuff."

"That's Pepper," she mused.

"Yeah. You know, it was really funny. I'd just come down in the elevator with the dog and Mrs. Emmons and Mimi."

"Uh-huh," June teased in a playful jealous put-on.

"Well, the dog was practically sneezing," Win continued. "And she kept swiveling her head in Mimi's direction, as if trying to tell me something."

"I wonder..." June started.

"What?"

"Oh, I don't know. Maybe we should pay another call on Mimi?"

"Aw, June, we're stepping on tricky ground here. At this point, half the people at the Plaza look suspicious to me. But we can't just barge in on people's lives without something substantial to go on. Sure, we have a million finger prints from the murder scene, and we could probably have a ball matching them up, but we can't go around testing everybody without cause."

June sat up straight, excited and affirmative. "Well, maybe we can *make* a cause! Mind if we do a little play acting, Win?"

Mellow with food and drink, he nodded, "Why not?"

She pursued her idea. "Concentrate now, OK?"

"I am." He smiled back.

"What could drive *you* to hurt, maybe kill, a harmless old lady?" she asked.

He laughed at the jolt of her question. "What if she wasn't harmless?" he countered.

"OK," she answered, "let's enter that into the factor, too. How about greed?"

"Hatred," he contributed. "Desperation."

"I'll go along with any of those," she said. "What about frustration? And just plain old-fashioned anger?"

"Revulsion? A fatal attraction?" he added, going along with the game.

"Now we're getting somewhere!" June exclaimed. "Who do we know who could feel so intensely?"

"Me?" Win grinned, playfully.

"Oh, don't be silly," she said, fondly.

They parted that night with a hug, a kiss, and plans to run on the trail tomorrow. New leads would just have to wait until Monday.

21
The Scare

For security reasons, the tri-level garage at the Park Plaza had been designed with locks galore. You needed a key to release the automatic gate and a second key to open the door on each floor inside the garage that led to the lobby and the elevator. Without that extra tool, there was no way to get into the living quarters of the building from the garage, although you could get *out* easily enough for a door on the ground level was never locked to pedestrians.

Nancy Webb had always thought this arrangement ridiculous. More than once she had gone to the garage to put something in her car and forgotten to take her entry key with her. The elevator door would clang shut behind her, and she'd be stranded until another tenant either drove into the garage or, happily, appeared from the elevator.

Other times, Nancy, whose space was on the lowest level and in the darkest corner, had simply walked up the ramp in considerable annoyance, left the garage through the pedestrian's door, and walked around to the front of the building to buzz Ruth to let her in.

But, Nancy had sometimes thought, *what if I hadn't been able to do that? What if I couldn't walk that far, like some of the old folks who live here? What if I was forced to stay in the garage until another tenant arrived? Why, I could be trapped down there for hours! And what if a person up to no good was already in the garage, hiding in the shadows, ready to pounce on a helpless person?*

Her fears came true late Saturday night.

Clad in her usual brief T-shirt and shorts, Nancy had driven to the Lucky Market for needs too heavy to carry. She'd taken Angus for company. He loved to ride shotgun.

It was a dark evening, her spirits were gloomy, and she was so eager to get home to the haven of the Plaza that she used her Genie for instant admission while still half a block away. Her parking space, one of the least desirable in the Plaza, had been assigned to her when she'd first moved in. Although she felt unsafe down there, she had never gotten around to requesting another.

She entered. Had her headlights picked out the shadow of someone lurking beside a car on the middle level as she swept down the ramp to the bottom? "Don't be silly," she said to herself. "Your nerves are just on edge because of what's happened here recently."

For no apparent reason, Angus chose that moment, as she pulled into her parking space and killed the engine, to begin barking.

"Quiet!" she ordered. Damn. His barking was so nerve-wracking!

The dog paid no attention to her, but persisted in barking, louder and sharper. Distracted, Nancy muttered to herself, "Keep calm. Just open the door. Have your building key ready. Get to the elevator. Go home. Do it! NOW!" It was then she discovered she'd forgotten her second key.

"Shit!" she sputtered, furious at herself. Scared, too, for hadn't a shape moved across the garage, where she thought she had seen something before?

She fumbled again in her purse, but was so agitated she dropped it, and in her haste to get out of the car let it lie. Angus, still intent on barking, did not follow her, and she slammed the car door, automatically locking both keys and Angus inside.

The dog barked madly now as she heard footsteps stalking nearer. She panicked. She turned to run up the ramp to the pedestrian exit, and was almost there when she was grabbed.

She tried to scream, but was too terrified to make more than a whimpering sound. "No! Please, no!" she cried, struggling to escape the strong hands that sought to rove her body.

Below, on the lower level, Angus was barking wildly, ineffectually trying to help.

She kicked, and managed to bite the intruder on his wrist. "Little bitch," he snarled, intent on rape.

But he was diverted by searching shafts of light as the garage door shuddered open. Seeing that a vehicle was about to enter, the would-be rapist escaped out the back door and into the dark, hiding night. Nancy, shaken, ran to greet the incomer.

"Help!" she screamed, her urgent cry fortified by Angus's shrill, distant barks.

The car braked quickly, and stopped. At the wheel was Merv. "There, there!" the huge man said, climbing from his van and putting his big meaty arm around her. "You're shivering!"

He took off his jacket, and wrapped it around her, like a child in a blanket. "We'd better call the police," Merv suggested.

"No!" Nancy protested. "The man is long gone by now. Besides, I couldn't identify him. I never saw his face.

"It was my fault anyway. I should have known to stay in the car and keep blowing the horn. Please! I don't want any fuss about this."

"But he could have harmed you," said Merv.

"Well, he didn't," she answered bluntly. "Please, Merv, let this be our little secret, okay?"

Angus, still below and barking to beat the band, reminded her to add, "I've gotta get my dog out of my car before he gets me evicted!"

"Don't worry about that, little lady," said Merv soothingly. "I'll stand up for you and your dog anytime."

"Thanks, Merv," she said, in calm control of herself once more. "But I *would* appreciate it if you'd walk me to Ruth's apartment. She has a spare set of my keys."

"I'll do better than that," he said. "I'll come back to the garage with you, just in case that creep is hanging around."

22
Salt and Pepper

"Going somewhere?" Helen Emmons smiled sweetly from her chosen perch—the most comfortable chair in the lobby. The angelic-faced grey-haired grandmother from the sixth floor adored Sundays.

She liked to rise early so as to go to the first mass at Saint Catherine. She would tiptoe out before her spaniel, Pepper, woke. Dressed in her Sunday best, she often met other dog walkers from the Plaza as she walked briskly along El Camino Real to the church at the corner of Bayswater.

"Good morning! I'll say a prayer for you!" she would gaily carol to each one in passing. And they would laugh, and wave, and go on their way.

After church, she would hurry home, conscience-stricken, to tend to Pepper's needs.

Carrying a pooper scooper in a paper bag, just in case of an accident enroute, she would lead the spaniel to the ivy beds of the Norsk Arms Apartments down the street. Mission accomplished, they'd go directly home but instead of riding upstairs she would settle herself in the lobby for the balance of the morning. It never occurred to Helen that she looked like a hawk, eyeing everyone coming in and out.

The spaniel lay at her feet, docile and resigned, a perpetual tear staining the corners of its eyes.

Sundays were great for people watching. Helen would

prefer to be in the bosom of her family, but her son and daughter rarely invited her to their homes anymore, except for obligatory holidays. Her "family" at the Plaza would just have to do.

Helen hated to be alone. She despised the sound of silence. Except on Sundays, the first thing she did every day upon waking was to turn on the radio, bringing music and voices into her rooms. Preferably big band dance music, although she was also fond of Streisand's beltier ballads.

A devout member of the lobby coffee klatsch, she was usually the first to arrive, beating even Laura, the acknowledged "hostess." But the coffee group did not meet on Sundays. It was up to Helen to entertain herself.

She had developed a Sunday routine of small talk, easily remembered light things to say to make contact with her neighbors. Although mere banalities, they usually evoked a friendly response. Sometimes a neighbor would even sit and visit a while. The "I'll say a prayer for you" was a standard remark. She also had the weather down pat. "It's nice out." (Or, "Was it nice out?" if they were coming in). "But you'll need" (or "You won't need," or "Did you need?") " . . . a sweater."

The time of day was predictable, too. Purposely, she never wore a watch so as to have an excuse to ask, "What time is it, please? . . . Oh my goodness, how the day is flying!"

As noon approached and before going upstairs for brunch, she had a follow-up quip to her greeting of earlier that morning. "I *said* a prayer for you!" she would chirp, cheerfully. Only a slight droop of Pepper's stubby tail betrayed the dog's boredom.

From Saint Paul's Episcopal Church, across the street from the Plaza, the bells chimed, tolling the hour. *Four o'clock and all is well,* Elsie's attacker giggled to himself.

What a nightmare last Monday had been. If only he could forget it. Since that fateful evening, he had been keeping himself exceptionally busy, playing hard, working hard, falling into bed exhausted. But he never slept well. He would wake, breathing heavily, heart pounding, pulse racing, at the undeniable realization, "My god, I killed her. Me!" He would lie, eyes closed, concentrating on blocking out his senses and his conscience until, incredibly, sleep returned, but troubled.

There was a time when Sundays had been his favorite day of the week. It was when he caught up on his paperwork and chores. But this Sunday he loathed. That old dame in the lobby had given him a jolt. What did she mean—she'd said a prayer for him? Did she know? Hell. He was reading too much into it. He just had too much time on his hands today for remembering...

My god, it was only a week ago! Why did Elsie have to be so goddamned unreasonable? It need not have happened. What difference did it make to her, anyway? Not having it was just a drop in the bucket for her. She could certainly spare it. She had no family to leave it to. He was the logical person to have it. Why couldn't she have seen that? Bah! What did the selfish old broad know, anyway, of ambition, longing, and the striving for excellence? She was just like all the other females in his life; stubborn, unyielding, impossible.

Of course, he hadn't meant for it to end violently, like that. He'd been just as astonished as she. Well, not quite "just as," he admitted nervously. But he wasn't a terrible person. Actually, he regarded himself as a mild-tempered guy, a veritable Mr. Clean.

All his life he had trod the straight and narrow. Done what was expected of him. Obeyed his parents. Gone to

Sunday school. Hugged his grandmother when told to on dutiful Sunday visits, although her chronic bad breath damn near made him throw up. When the kids at school had done childish and stupid acts of vandalism, he had looked the other way. Stayed clean. Not participated. Later, at jobs, he had pretended not to care or notice when promotions went to others not as qualified as he. Ass kissing might be a way of life for many, but never for him. When called for military service, he had gone—not evaded Korea like every other young man he knew. He voted Republican. Paid his alimony on time.

Swallowing the last of his second Scotch, he grinned with another rueful thought. Why, he had never even gotten a traffic ticket! All his life, until last Monday, he had been a model citizen.

OK, he admitted, looking at his empty glass, so maybe I have a slight drinking problem. But I need this booze to sharpen my thinking, to be original. What the hell . . . why not . . .

He rose to mix himself another drink and resettled on the sunny patio with an open magazine on his lap.

He couldn't concentrate. Damn. His inner voice was nagging again. Why did you do it? *Why? Why? Why?*

"Oh, shut up," he muttered at his private demons, flipping a page so sharply it ripped.

If only Elsie hadn't been so whiny . . . just like his mother, his sisters, his aunts . . . And, yes, his grandmother . . . Even his live-in friend could be a whiner, he mused, glancing into the living room at the tousle-haired creature curled up, napping, on the couch.

Would he have lost his head that night, he wondered, if Elsie Johnson had been a man and not a woman? Would that same awful red-burning feeling have crept up his spine and taken over his brain? If it had been anyone but her, with her exasperating ways, would the blind rage still have consumed him?

Facing the devil within himself, he realized, with a start, yes, it probably would have happened, be it man or woman. For this was something he had to have. *Had* to. It represented the all-important goal of his life; his big chance to follow in the footsteps of the masters, savor their trials, taste their triumphs.

He shivered, reliving the evening that had begun so innocently, and ended with such awful finality. Perhaps he should have come forward immediately? He could have claimed it was an accident. Maybe it wasn't too late now? Hell, they'd never believe him.

The natural thing to do that night had been to run and hope that her death would be accepted as "natural." After all, she was elderly. Probably had a bum heart. She had to die sometime. Didn't everyone?

He hadn't counted on a detective coming into the picture. The persistence of the man and the female cop and that dog, that damn staring dog, had definitely caught him off guard.

He'd been careful in talking with them. There was no way they could know. Or was there? Perhaps, when things blew over, he could move away. Get out of town. Make a new life for himself. Hell, the rent here was getting to be too high, anyway. He needed to forget.

His inner voice spoke to him again. "You're going to be caught, you know."

"I suppose so," he mumbled to himself.

"Here's to you, old girl," he said out loud, raising his glass in rueful toast to the memory of Elsie.

His friend in the other room stirred, and woke, alarmed at the drunken tone of his voice.

23
Sunday

True to their plans upon parting Saturday night, Win had picked up June at 6:30 Sunday morning and they were on the trail, running, by 7:00. Chief had the day off, also. But since dogs are not allowed on the trail, he stayed home, perfectly content. He always found it enjoyable to have the house to himself and wander through the rooms, flopping wherever he liked.

It was a glorious morning on the trail. Faint wisps of fog from the Pacific drifted dreamily over the mountains. Seagulls, cawing, exuberantly wheeled in the bright blue sky. On the water, colonies of ducks paddled in large, lazy circles. A light wind ruffled the lake.

June and Win chatted easily as they jogged along.

"This must have been some kind of heaven way back when it was a Spanish land grant," she said.

He agreed. Even the poison oak looked beautiful. They ran to the four-mile marker, wheeled around, and were heading back when a buck and a doe sprang from the woods and leapt across their path. They laughed with delight at the sudden encounter.

"Wonder if we look as attractive to them?" June said.

"I'm sure of it!" Win replied.

Because Sunday was his usual day to be there, many other runners recognized him and nodded in passing. Win noticed, proudly, the approving looks they gave his lovely companion.

By the time they had returned to the starting gate, traffic on the trail had become congested. Bikers, roller bladers, runners, walkers, all jockeyed for elbow room.

"Bet they'd clear out in a hurry if they knew this had once been bear country!" June joked.

The drive home led past the Crystal Springs Golf Course. Its roller-coaster hills and verdant valleys teemed with golfers. Without thinking, Win eased his foot off the pedal, allowing the car to coast slowly along the perimeters of the golf course. "I'd like to be out there," he remarked idly.

She shot him a "Hey! What do you mean!" sort of glance. He caught it.

"Oh, not today!" He grinned back at her. "Never on Sunday!"

He stepped on the gas. They crossed the 280 freeway. After the roundabout on Hayne, they zig-zagged from the street named Barbara to Ralston to Laurent and plunged down Chateau Drive, which always reminded him of a ski jump, to the flatlands of Burlingame. It wasn't the fastest way home, but it was the prettiest.

"How about coming in for some coffee?" she asked, as they pulled up before her house.

"You're a mind reader!" he answered.

I hope he doesn't have plans for the rest of the day, she thought. *I really like being with this man.*

At the sound of the key grating in the latch, Chief bounded to the door to greet them.

"Hi, boy!" Win said, reaching to give him an affectionate scratch behind the ears.

"Did anybody phone?" June asked the dog, fondly.

Chief grinned at her, his broom of a tail wagging madly.

The threesome went into the kitchen. June measured out the grounds, clicked on the percolator, and the wonderful aroma of fresh-brewing coffee soon filled the room.

"Like a cinnamon bun?" she asked, cutting the string off the distinctive pink box from Ingeborg's Bakery.

He wasn't about to refuse anything she had to offer. "Thanks!" he said, taking two.

She poured the coffee and they sipped from mugs, slowly and leisurely, savouring the hot fragrant taste. Chief looked up at them, hopefully.

"It's such a nice day. Let's take him for a walk," Win suggested.

"You *are* a jock, aren't you!" she said, teasingly. "Eight miles of running not enough for you?"

Her spirits were light and gay at the knowledge that yes, obviously, they would be spending more of the day together.

Clipping on Chief's long leash, she lit out the door. Win followed. They set off at a brisk pace, the dog gracefully trotting alongside. They headed toward Hillsborough and the roads that border the fairways of the Burlingame Country Club. The sidewalks there were like country lanes, unpaved, of natural dirt. Meandering foot paths paralleled the roads leading through the posh residential district. Huge elms and oak trees overhung the paths. Branches overlapped picturesquely. The effect was like an arboretum.

Tongue lolling happily, Chief led them from Sharon Drive onto Eucalpytus. He suddenly slowed, turning his head and pointing his ears. Win and June followed the motion.

There, across the street, before the black iron gates of a long impressive driveway leading to a gleaming white mansion, stood Merv, the big guy from the Plaza. Garbed in a brown uniform, he was an imposing sight, officiously helping the Hillsborough police control traffic to a private party. He was double-checking invitations, opening the gates to most cars, keeping them closed to some.

"No gate crasher's going to get past him!" Win remarked, amused.

"That's for sure," June agreed.

If Merv noticed them, he gave no sign. They, too, pretended indifference, and continued with their walk.

Turning the corner to June's home, Win suggested, "Would you like to see where I live?"

She would, indeed.

They climbed into his car, Chief springing into the backseat.

Win's apartment was a mile away, a modest duplex on Capuchino Avenue, in the area of Burlingame called Broadway.

"Welcome to my humble abode!" he said, opening the door to his second-floor walkup.

It certainly is, she thought. Just an uninspired clutch of rooms looking out on the street and the apartment house next door. It was haphazardly furnished. Simply a place to hang your hat. No homey feeling at all. *Well, at least, he keeps it neat,* she thought appreciatively.

She gazed about the living room, curious to see his taste in possessions. On one wall, a poorly framed old-fashioned print of golfers flailing away in a Scottish landscape. On another hung a crude cartoon of a golfer missing the ball completely. On the table were the magazines *Golf Digest, Golf World,* and just plain *Golf.*

In the bookcase, *Driving the Green, The World's Best Golf, Golf Facts and Feats, The Concise Dictionary of Golf, A World Portrait of Golf, Golf in the Kingdom . . .* Golf this, golf that.

"You sure have a one-track mind!" she said kiddingly.

"I do!" he agreed, joining her by the bookcase. "This

one's my favorite. Practically my Bible."

He took from the shelf a large, heavy volume, *The Architects of Golf*, and handed it to her.

She feigned interest and, as seemed to be expected of her, flipped through the pages. "Oh, isn't this nice!" she exclaimed vaguely. "What a lot of pictures!"

He didn't have to be much of a detective to see that her mind was not on golf. Gently, he took the book from her and laid it on a table.

There was a moment of silence, and then: "Say, I feel a bit raunchy," he said. "Would you mind if I took a quick shower? That is," he added, with a hopeful grin, "if I can invite myself to spend the rest of the afternoon with you. I thought we might go back to your place."

She thought that was a great idea. Certainly, her home was far cozier than his for pursuing this budding courtship.

"Go!" she smiled.

"I'll be out in a minute." He disappeared down the hall to his bedroom and bath.

A few seconds later, she caught a quick glimpse of his lean naked body as he ducked into the bathroom. He hadn't bothered with a robe.

What a tease! she thought.

While he showered, she curled up on the sofa and pored through the book he'd called his Bible. She smiled as she heard him cheerfully whistling while the water ran hard, and then stopped.

A few minutes later, he was back. She looked up approvingly at his casual garb of pullover sweater and jeans. He had a nice piney smell about him, and his sandy hair was still damp from the shower. They returned to her house. Then it was her turn to bathe, which she did quickly, jealous of the moments not spent with him.

That afternoon, they settled down like an old married

couple, watching a professional golf tournament on television. To her surprise, June did not find it boring at all. The grace, the good looks, the saucy buns-out posture of so many of the handsome young golfers, held her attention.

"Is this a 'penal' course?" she asked him mischievously during the telecast. She had found the common golf description funny while browsing through his "Bible," and let it unwrap deliciously from her tongue, prompting a surprised—and pleased—reaction from Win.

"As a matter of fact, it is!" he said.

Afterward, they phoned to Round Table Pizza for home-delivered supper. And when it was finished, they sat closely together. He slung his arm casually along the back of the sofa, just barely, tantalizingly, touching her.

Discovering they were both "Murder, She Wrote" fans, they tuned it in, and chuckled at their inability as professional police persons to outguess Jessica Fletcher in the convoluted plot.

When it was over, Win excused himself. The night was still young, but they had much to do tomorrow. Warmly, they kissed good night, their tongues teasingly flicking. How relaxing it had been not to have talked shop all day! Just the way Sundays should be.

24
Merv

It was nine o'clock sharp Monday morning, and June, Win, and Chief were back on the job at the Plaza.

"Anything interesting happen since we last saw you?" Win asked Laura.

"Only Mr. Allen rolling home five sheets to the wind on Saturday!" she laughed.

"I hear he caused a bit of a row on the avenue," she added.

"Oh, really?" said Win. "What about."

Thanks to a passionate interest in food and drink, Merv Allen was a blimp of a man, carrying an enormous paunch of a stomach. Most tenants liked him, however. Although he seemed rough and uncouth, he had a gentle side, as he had evidenced Saturday night in the garage when he'd gone to Nancy's rescue.

Merv had a constant smile for the ladies, a hearty "Hi" for the men. The dogs at the Plaza were crazy about him for, like poor dead Elsie, he could always be counted on for a handout. But behind his gimlet eyes, magnified clown-like behind tri-focal, old-fashioned wire-rimmed glasses lurked a sullen personality.

Merv supported himself by catering dinner parties throughout the peninsula and moonlighting as a private security guard. He was ambiguous about the guard work. He did it because it paid well, and he was always on the shorts. But he would far prefer to stay full-time in the kitchen. On the other hand, he liked the power that the guard jobs gave him.

Awkward and clumsy in his everyday clothes, Merv in uniform felt like the boss of the roost, the king of the jungle. And he was very light on his big flat feet. A person arousing his ire would never know what hit them. He could move—and strike—that fast.

Merv's guard jobs satisfied a need to dominate that he had learned to like as a child, defending himself in bully attacks against "the fat boy." As an adult, he suppressed his aggression most of the time. But he enjoyed letting it surface now and then and watching the surprise on people's faces. Merv had been married once. Not for long. His wife had been unwilling and even afraid to cope with his wild mood swings of nice guy/mean guy. Nearing fifty, he craved affection, but on his own terms. He had a lady friend who slept over now and then.

He had been attracted to the Park Plaza because of its "family feeling" and because it permitted pets. His choice of pet was a singing canary that he allowed to fly free within his apartment. The bird was fluttering around the kitchen now, as he slapped out slabs of dough, sending puffs of whiteness in clouds above the stove.

Barefoot, as he always was at home, Merv was in his element doing what he loved best; baking bread. His huge chef's apron was splattered with flour, sugar, yeast, and spices. He was so content he was singing along with the bird, imitating its song and chuckling at its fluted reply, when his doorbell rang.

It crossed his mind that it might be his buddy, the bartender at the Bit of England, coming to apologize for throwing him out on Saturday. *Hell,* Merv thought, looking back on the day. *All I did was help myself to a few bucks from his till. He should have known I'd pay it back. Of course it might be awhile . . .*

Gad! What a hangover he'd had yesterday! And having to work that lunch job had been murder. He shrugged and gave the dough another violent punch. He wiped his hands on his apron and went to the door.

Genial grin on his face, expecting to see his pal, he threw open the door. He stepped back, grin gone. The detective, the policewoman, and the police dog stood there.

"May we come in?" Harry Winslow asked.

Reluctantly, Merv answered, "Gee, I'm awful busy."

"It's just routine, Mr. Allen," Win said. "We'll only be a minute."

Sensing that to argue would be futile, Merv stepped aside. "Be my guest," he mumbled as they entered.

They stayed more than a minute, and their questions were hardly "just routine."

"What happened Saturday in the town?" (Although they already knew from Laura's report of what Mr. Chin had told her. Win and June had made a hasty visit to the Bit of England, where they'd found the bartender happy to talk.)

Merv gave his version. "It was a misunderstanding. I borrowed some money from a friend, that's all."

Win smiled, condescendingly. Then he asked, as if out of the blue, "How well did you know Mrs. Johnson?"

"Not well," Merv said, evasively.

"When did you last see her?" from June.

"I dunno," he shrugged.

"What did you talk about with her?" Win persisted.

Suddenly, Merv opened up. It was as if he was anxious to get a load off his mind.

"Oh, hell, I might as well tell you," he offered. "You'd have found out anyway."

Sitting alertly, Chief's eyes rolled, his tail slowly twitching, as he watched the canary flying about the room. Win and June stared intently at Merv, who told his story.

"I have a dream, see?"

Catering dinner parties was all very well, he explained. He delved briefly into specifics; after all, food was the love of his life. And you never knew who might be his next customers. These two, perhaps? His best menus revolved around beef. Short ribs, Mandarin style, stroganoff with dill weed, pot roast, prime rib, roulades. He also worked from the menus of the masters. He had an extensive collection of cookbooks. They filled a bookcase in his living room, and he pointed out his favorites—Craig Claiborne, James Beard, Marcella Hazen, Jacques Pepin, Waverly Root, Rene Verdon, Escoffier, Julia Child . . . They were all there. He loved adding his own embellishments to their recipes. He also catered to the current craze for low-calorie pastas, he told Win and June.

His phone rang often with orders for birthday cakes and pastries. Even the owners of the Plaza were customers, with a standing order for his Yule Log traditionally featured at their Christmas party. But what Merv really wanted to do was bake bread. Gourmet bread. If Nancy's Quiche, based in nearby Palo Alto, could become a national success, so, he reasoned, could his "Breads to Die For."

Ever since he had thought of the name, the dream had been growing within him. For years he had been experimenting with various bread recipes. He had sifted them down to five different kinds and, booming with enthusiasm, had developed the habit in recent weeks of banging on doors within the Plaza, passing out delicious samples and asking for critiques.

There was a dollars-and-cents reason for this generosity. Merv wanted to go big-time and sell his breads in all the best stores. It would take money, lots of money, to build a professional bakery, hire the help, and market his wares. A weakness for betting on horses during the Bay Meadows five-month race season had obliterated what little savings he had. His credit was the pits. He couldn't get a bank loan. What he needed was an angel. Someone or more than one person to bankroll him.

For about a year, he had been on the lookout for a wealthy person to back him in what he knew could become a tremendous success. Better than Nancy's Quiche, even! "When I met Elsie Johnson, I thought I had it made."

"So, she wouldn't help you?" prompted Win.

"Hell, no. All the money that old bag had, and she wouldn't lend me a penny," Merv snarled.

"What made you so sure she had money?" pressed Win.

"I saw her checkbook," Merv admitted.

"How did you do that?" June asked.

Merv sighed, shifting his bulky body in reluctant anticipation of the answer he was about to give. "This one night she invited me to her place. I was going to come right out with it and ask her for a loan for my business. But I wanted to be sure she was as rich as I thought she was. So I went to her desk while she was in the kitchen and fished around and found her checkbook. I had a good look. She had a ton of money, all right. She'd have made a really good investment in me. Unfortunately, she didn't see it that way."

Merv went on. "I never got a chance to explain my deal. You see, she came out of the kitchen real sudden like. When she saw me with her checkbook, she threw me out.

It's getting to be a habit," he chortled, thinking of the incident at the bar on Saturday.

Neither policeperson smiled.

Merv hesitated to say more, catching the knowing glances they were exchanging. "But, hey!" Merv added, throwing up his hands. "That wasn't the night she was killed! That happened weeks ago. Honest!"

"Can you prove it?" Win demanded.

"Matter of fact, I can," said Merv. "When I was coming home in the elevator that night, I ran into Nancy Webb. You know, the Scottie's owner?" He would have liked to make himself look good by telling about his rescuing her in the garage. But true to his pledge of silence, he didn't. Instead, he said, "You can also ask Mr. Chin about me. He'd remember. I tried my pitch on him the same night."

"We'll talk to them all right," Win informed him. "Thanks for your help. Oh, and by the way, please don't leave town."

"I wasn't planning to," Merv retorted, rising to his feet with surprising lightness, eager to show them out. He offered a friendly handshake.

They were struck by the strength of his hands. Strong enough to strangle? Easily.

Merv's handshake to Win was merely masculine, but to June he gave a bone-crusher. Poker-faced, she countered with a special hurting pressure of her own, causing Merv to wince.

They departed, with the dog at their heels.

Out of the corner of his eye, Chief shot a reluctant glance at leaving Merv's yellow bird, still flying around.

25
The Key

"*Now* what?" June asked, looking at Win intently.

"Patience!" he chided. "Let's go to the Johnson apartment. There has to be something we've missed."

He fumbled in his pants pocket. Then in the other one. "Rats. Where in blazes did I put that key?"

"You gave it to me to hold. Don't you remember?" June smiled sweetly. "Here!" And she passed it over.

"Thanks! What would I do without you?" he said, with a grateful wink.

As they entered the elevator, Mimi stepped out and smiled cordially at them.

Blithe and carefree, Mimi strolled to the Lucky Market. She only intended to buy a carton of milk. Inevitably, unable to resist temptations along the aisles, she left the store with a bulging load of groceries. She could scarcely see over the top of the paper bag as she strolled the short block back to the Plaza.

She set the parcel on the doormat and fished in her fanny pack for her key. Pursing her lips, she rummaged about, disturbing cash, credit cards, checkbook, pen, notebook, lipstick, comb. Damn it, no keys. It was not the first time she had forgotten them. And it certainly would not be the last.

Randomly, she stabbed at various buzzers. Always before, someone would return the buzz that opened the door without bothering to ask who was there. When the door was released, she would sweep inside and up to her floor where she kept a spare key to her apartment on the back of the hallway table. Since Elsie's death, however, tenants were being more cautious. Nobody buzzed her in today.

Through the glass door, Mimi could see Laura at her desk in the office. She rapped on the glass to get her attention. Politely at first; then in angry bursts.

Mimi was studiously ignored. Feigning important business on the phone, Laura was in one of her stubborn moods. It was Laura's belief that if you couldn't remember to keep your key with you at all times, tough luck. She wasn't a doorman. Damned if she'd allow careless tenants to take advantage of her. With so many people living under the same roof, she could easily be put in the position of having to jump to their bidding all day long on the nuisance matter of lockouts.

Soon after assuming her job, she had had two signs printed. One she had posted by the call buttons outside the building, the other at her office door. They disclaimed the manager's responsibility for providing duplicate keys except in dire emergency. Shut-outs were directed to Burlingame's only locksmith.

At thirty-five dollars per service call, Pete Graves, locksmith, had a lucrative thing going with the Plaza. There was some speculation among some of the tenants that he gave a cut of his earnings to Laura.

In any event, his service was excellent as Mimi found when, resignedly, she walked back to the market to phone him. The locksmith was just pulling up to the Plaza as she returned. Only it wasn't middle-aged, pot-bellied Pete Graves this time, but a new assistant—a slim young man in hip-hugging jeans and a rakish grin.

What a hunk! After he let her into the lobby, she told

him she needed his services to unlock her apartment door too. Pointedly ignoring Laura, who in turn pretended not to notice *her,* Mimi led the young man into the elevator. She smiled in anticipation of a possible romantic entanglement to come.

On the sixth floor, she strode past the table where her spare key was hidden. She stood, helplessly, before her door to 605. "Here we are," she smiled, with a come-hither lilt to her voice.

The key man bent to his task. But Mimi's design for sex did not happen. Her intercom was buzzing as she and the locksmith entered her apartment.

"Yes?" Mimi said into it, annoyed at this interruption.

"Hello—Mimi?" a familiar voice sputtered. "It's me, Laura. Did you get in all right?"

"Obviously," Mimi answered, sarcastically. She resisted the impulse to add "No thanks to you." It was smart to stay on Laura's good side.

"Can I speak to Pete's man, please?" Laura piped.

Stepping aside, Mimi gestured to the handsome young locksmith. "She wants *you.*"

"Hello?" he spoke into the box.

"It's me, the manager. I'm outside the building. I came out to water the plants.

"Buzz me in, will you? And I want you to meet me at the door to my office."

"Pardon?" he answered, bewildered at this turn of events.

"Now!" she snapped. "Goddammit," her voice shouted over the intercom, picking up the incomprehension in his voice. "I don't have my keys with me! I've locked myself out."

"Serves her right!" Mimi exclaimed, bursting into laughter.

26
Sidetracked

Up and down. Down and up.

Stella Rankin of apartment 507 had been slinking about more than usual and riding the elevator conspicuously often. Since she was known for keeping to herself and making only spartan use of the lift—twice a day, at most—her sudden change of behavior was the talk of the building. The coffee klatsch was particularly intrigued. Among themselves they discussed what possible meaning to attach to the trancelike expression on her face and the mysterious clipboard she kept in her hand.

What was she up to? Nobody dared ask her. Besides, it was more fun to speculate. Maybe she was plotting something evil? She certainly was the type, they nervously laughed among themselves.

Also curious was the little mutt, Millie, who lived across the hall. It amused the dog to keep track of Stella's wanderings by plastering itself prone at the door and peering through the crack beneath. A million times, or so it seemed, the woman went to the trash room. That in itself seemed strange. Millie's mistress, Ruth Kenny, never did that so often. How many sacks of rubbish could one person have?

On Tuesday, upon being brought home after her noon walk, the dog noticed Stella's door slightly ajar. She seized the opportunity. Breaking away from Ruth, the dog wriggled, leash trailing, into Stella's apartment. Ruth, startled and chagrined at the dog's boldness, froze for a moment. It was all the time the dog needed to dart about, investigating.

For a creature that loved to run and jump, the living room was paradise. It was empty of furniture; only artists' easels, five of them, on stands around the room. Their brace bars made them inviting to leap through, like hurdles, which the little dog did, one after another.

Her curiosity satisfied there, she was off like a shot to the bedroom. No fun and games in that room. The dog pulled up short, disinterested at the bare furnishings. Just a bed, a small chest that doubled as a bedside table, a floor-to-ceiling mirror. Plus a sort of shrine in one corner, with votive candles emitting a heady incense. Displayed before them were the most treasured keepsakes of Stella's haunted youth—a pressed gardenia, a dance card, a teddy bear, a school yearbook.

"Oh, my goodness," exclaimed Ruth, who had recovered her wits, rushed into the apartment, and was about to grab Millie.

"Seen enough?" a low monotone voice sounded behind her. Stella had returned from the trash room.

"Oh, I'm so sorry!" blurted Ruth. "My dog . . ."

"I have eyes," Stella said sharply.

Anxious to appease the woman, Ruth hurriedly said, with honest amazement, "You're an artist!"

"Trying to be," Stella answered, in a halfway friendly tone.

In all the years she'd lived at the Plaza, no one had ever shown the slightest interest in how she filled her days. Or so she thought. It had never occurred to her that she put people off with her weird ways of behaving.

"May I look at your paintings?" Ruth asked. She knew she'd be late getting back to work this day, but it was marvelous to have cracked the armor of this strange neighbor. She yearned to know more.

"Why that's me!" she reacted with surprise at the watercolor portrait on the first easel she stopped at. In the picture, her hair was styled better and her chin was firmer, but it was her all right. It was the first flattering likeness she'd ever seen of herself. "When did you do it?"

"I've been studying you for a long time," Stella replied. "I like your cheekbones. Matter of fact, I started with you."

"You *what?*" Ruth reacted, mystified.

"When I decided to take up portrait painting," explained Stella, "I needed a model, but I was too embarrassed to ask anybody. And I couldn't afford to pay anyone. So I just memorized faces of people here in the building who'd been decent to me. You always were."

"But we thought you wanted to be alone!" cried Ruth.

"Not really," Stella answered, shyly.

To fill the awkward silence, Ruth moved to the second painting. "This is *very* good," she said, admiringly. "It's Detective Winslow, right?"

"Oh, and here's his partner," she said, moving on to the third easel. "*Very* nice." She stood back, to appreciate the subtleties of Stella's skill.

"When did you ever find time to do them?" Ruth asked.

"I've been trailing them lately," Stella admitted. "Whenever I saw them, I made notes to jog my memory."

(*Oh,* thought Ruth. *So that explains all the elevator trips and the clipboard.*)

"I threw a lot of my bad starts away," Stella went on. "That's what I was doing when you came in. I can't stand having my artwork around if it isn't the best I can do. You think they'd be pleased with these?" she asked, modestly.

"I do," breathed Ruth. "They're lovely. What will you do with them when you've finished?"

"I don't know," said Stella. "Just give them away, I guess."

"I bet you could sell them," Ruth suggested, thinking to herself, *This gal's a genius! Maybe I could become her agent!*

"What else do you do?" Ruth asked, conversationally.

"I write poems," Stella blandly replied. "And I like to compose crossword puzzles."

Ruth was at the fourth canvas now where she stood quiet for a moment, confused and apprehensive. "Isn't this Elsie Johnson?"

"Yes," Stella acknowledged.

To Ruth's imagination, the yes had a sinister hiss.

"I finished it just before she died," Stella said. "I'm sorry I never had a chance to show it to her." A tear trickled down her cheek.

Ruth recoiled, alarmed.

Still in her introspective mood, Stella went on with her thoughts. "She was a lovely lady. She's the only one in this building who ever invited me to her home. That was only once, but I've never forgotten. She had so many beautiful things. I loved looking at them. Especially the treasures in the armoire. They were so good to the touch. I don't know why she never invited me back. Anyway, the one time I was there was a wonderful evening, and I wanted to remember her just the way she looked that night."

Having heard the details of how Elsie was dressed when she was found, Ruth was relieved to note that in the painting Elsie's sweater was blue.

"And who," Ruth asked, moving on to the last canvas, "is *this*?"

"That's Cat," Stella said proudly.

Hearing his name, a gorgeous mink-brown Abyssinian ambled out from the kitchen. Spying Millie, it crept toward her, pantherlike.

"I think we'd better be going!" Ruth said, hustling her dog out the door.

The cat, disappointed to lose a potential playmate, boxed the air with a frustrated paw.

27
The Date

It was now Wednesday, and for the third time in five days Win was at June's for dinner. He had invited her to dine at his favorite restaurant, the Alpine Inn, but she had declined. Not that she didn't like the charming basement hideaway, she hastened to add. She did, very much. "But I'd rather put my feet up at home, wouldn't you?" she had said. "If you would feel better about it," she had added, "why don't you bring a steak?" He had.

They were in the kitchen. Win was seasoning the meat—easy on the garlic, mostly just lemon-pepper. June was slicing mixings for an avocado and tomato salad. Chief sat, smiling, watching them, thumping the floor with his tail.

June was in a lemon yellow jumpsuit that set off her curves and her sunny disposition. The difference in their ages seemed to have vanished. Win had a spring to his step, a spark in his eyes, that hadn't been there for years.

Since giving themselves a day off on Sunday, they had longed to touch each other. She could still taste the warmth of his kiss. "Harry." It was the first time she had used his given name, and he warmed to the way she spoke it.

"Have you ever been in the Whistling Swan?" she said.

"The antique store on Primrose?" he asked.

The thought crossed his mind that she might be about to hint for a present. They were fast approaching that stage in their relationship. He had better pay attention.

"Yuh. I was there briefly yesterday," she answered. "You know, it's amazing how many tiny things there are that cost a whole lot of money."

"You're thinking about the case, aren't you?" he responded, relieved that a gift was not on her mind. He'd been feeling a little strapped for cash lately. He looked at her brightly.

She nodded, setting the paring knife aside.

"We need a motive, right?" she said.

He waggled his head, "Yes."

"Well, Harry, what if Mrs. Johnson was murdered for something she owned? Something valuable that she didn't bother to hide—that she kept in plain sight for anyone to see?"

"You know, you're getting to be pretty good at this sleuthing!" he said, kiddingly. "What sort of things caught your eye in that shop?"

"So many," she said wistfully. "Hand-painted demitasses. Cream pitchers. Fancy thimbles. Butcher weights. Snuff jar. Watchholders."

He laughed. She looked like a kid in a candy store.

She continued, reciting from memory other objects she'd admired. "There was an inkwell. Probably seventeenth century. A dinner bell. China figurines."

"Whoa!" he chuckled. "I get the picture. All the sort of stuff the victim had in her apartment, right?"

"Right!" June exclaimed. "Like we've seen on her tables, her bureau, her desk."

"And," Win added thoughtfully, "in that large armoire in her living room."

"Yes!" she said, excitedly. "There, especially!"

"But we've already looked there," he pointed out. "Nothing seemed out of place when we were there Monday."

"I know," she admitted.

"Still," he said, "you may be right. Tomorrow morning, first thing, we'll go back to the apartment and nose around again."

"Now, what do you say we eat? There's nothing like a new lead to whet the appetite!"

It was then the shuddering started. They looked apprehensively at each other. Chief sprang to his feet, cocking his head, ears pointed at full attention, quizzical expression on his face, trying to figure out this new experience.

The sound came first. A distant roar, like a faraway train, grinding closer and closer, louder and louder, and suddenly becoming quite deafening.

EARTHQUAKE!

The walls trembled, the floor seemed to roll like the deck of a ship in a rough sea. Lurching in the crazily gyrating room, Win and June reached for each other in mutual assurance. He grabbed her hand, and they staggered to the shelter of the closest doorway—the most supportive part of the house.

Earthquakes come with the territory in the San Francisco Bay area. They never last long—usually only seconds. But the chaos they can create is awesome.

Bridges can collapse. Freeways sometimes buckle. Buildings have caved in. Houses can be knocked off their foundations. Clocks stop. Hills split open with deep, yawning cracks. And with people, the effect is always the same. Sheer terror at the power of the forces of underground nature.

There isn't a darn thing you can do in an earthquake except take cover, hope that the damage will be slight, and pray you'll get out alive.

As always happened, the power went off. June's little house was plunged into darkness. The stove quit. The hum of the refrigerator fell silent. The flickering image on the TV screen vanished. The radio music cut off rudely in the middle of a love song. The windows rattled. From Saint Paul's church, the bells chimed. Just once. And as abruptly as it had begun, the great shaking stopped.

It had been less than twenty seconds, and, they would learn later, just a moderate six on the Richter scale, the logarithmic way by which seismologists all over the world can instantaneously measure the amount of energy released by an earthquake that's just happened. It's called the Richter scale after Prof. Charles Richter of the California Institute of Technology in Pasadena, who devised the system in 1935.

A six on the Richter scale is slight compared with the most famous quake in San Francisco history, the one of April 18, 1906, guesstimated to have been an 8.3. That one damn near destroyed the city and was the impetus for residential development to move out of San Francisco, south to Burlingame, and beyond.

A six is also nothing compared with the ferociousness of the 7.1 tremor of October 17, 1989, called Loma Prieta—Black Hill—after the peak in the Santa Cruz mountains beneath which it centered. That one, beginning eleven miles below the earth, erupted to within four miles of the surface, its violence causing awful damage in the Marina district of San Francisco. Part of the San Francisco-Oakland Bay Bridge had fallen down, crushing a number of motorists.

This was nothing like that. Still, a six on the Richter is a terrifying shake, and Win and June continued to stand in an embrace in the kitchen doorway of the dark and silent house. Chief remained rooted where he was, stockstill, trying to figure out what the heck had happened.

"Boy! That was a big one!" Win exclaimed. There was a sigh of relief in his voice, for the house was intact, their lives were safe.

"Why, you're trembling!" he suddenly realized.

She was, but from arousement by the nearness of him as much as fright of the quake.

She whispered something.

"What did you say, honey?"

"I'd really like it if you'd stay with me tonight," she said again, softly.

He stepped back, held her at arm's length, and looked solemnly into her yearning brown eyes. "My darling," he said huskily. "Are you sure?"

Even in the darkness, she was radiant, glowing, a woman alive with desire and longing.

Arms about each other, they found their way to her bedroom. Modestly, she closed the door on Chief, who had begun to follow them in. "Not tonight!" she said to the dog.

Understandingly, Chief flopped to the floor, keeping guard, outside their room of passion.

Along El Camino Real, the utility poles swayed and the street lights went out. The traffic lights, too. All was dark along the streets, except for the cars' piercing headlights eerily picking their way through the blackness.

The moment the quake had struck, many motorists had pulled to the side of the road and leapt out to look at their tires, thinking they must have a flat.

A few people burst outdoors, panic-stricken, from their homes and apartments. Some glanced fearfully behind them, expecting to see their buildings come crumbling down into rubble.

At Bits and Pieces, the town's pricey china and glassware shop proved to have a prophetic name. There was a sickening shattering as Baccarat crystal and Lenox plates topped from display shelves and smashed on the floor.

At the Park Plaza, much of the water in the swimming pool erupted onto the lawn.

A hairline crack rent a kitchen wall in Mary Hudson's second-floor apartment.

In Helen Emmons' bathroom on six, molding along the ceiling broke apart and rippled, as if a colony of spiders had spun instant webs.

In apartment 307, a heavy teak bookcase came crashing down, its books tumbling all over the floor. Christine Conrad would have a heck of a mess confronting her when she returned from her European trip on Friday.

In 308, Elsie's place, the quake had caused the glass doors to her antique cabinet to jostle open. She had kept what she called "knickknacks" there. Pricey things, small things, collected not only personally during her lifetime, but inherited from her parents. Elsie had never believed in safety deposit vaults. "No siree," she had explained to visitors startled to spot some obviously precious object in plain unguarded view. "If I can't see and touch things and enjoy them, why have them?"

28
Aftershocks

All about town, the great convulsion that had begun seven miles below the earth's surface and a hundred miles away, left its calling cards. Here a shattered window, there a tumbled chimney, and chaos at the Lucky Market, where it looked as if a mob had run amuck down the aisles, hurling cans, bottles, jars, and boxes to the floor in fits of rages.

The Park Plaza was in total darkness, and both elevators were out of order. Judging from the absence of calls for help, no one had been trapped riding in them, Laura noted, relieved. She scurried to the storeroom behind the mailboxes to grab what she called her "emergency box." It contained flashlights, candles, matches, a blanket, paper cups, a jug of water, and a transistor radio. She lugged it to the lobby, and busied herself at placing candles on the seven tables scattered around the room.

One never knew how long a blackout would last. It might be just an hour or so. Then again, the lights could be out all night, or longer. Either way, Laura knew from previous experience that there would be aftershocks—many minor rumblings and shakings, not likely to cause damage but scary all the same. Candles would be a lot more dependable than electricity.

She expected more than half of her tenants to soon make their way downstairs. Few who lived alone cared to wait in shaky solitude in their dark apartments. Of course one could always go to bed. But it was a little early in the evening for that.

Hurriedly moving about, Laura lit the candles. One by one they flickered cheerfully into life. By the time she had lit the seventh, the room had a warm, welcoming glow... *Like the setting for a party,* she thought with a satisfied smile.

She didn't have long to wait. Helen and Mimi were the first to arrive. Helen cradled the spaniel, Pepper, like a baby in her arms. Mimi, holding a flashlight, kept a helpful, guiding hand on the older woman's elbow. They had inched along the pitch black hall on their floor, and climbed down the six flights of stairs. As they passed each floor, other neighbors fell in behind. Each stepped, blinking, from the dark stairwell into the dancing light of the lobby.

"Welcome!" Laura shouted, determined to make the best of the situation. "I have potato chips and pretzels! Help yourselves!"

It was, after all, the dinner hour, and, although ovens and stoves were no longer operable, there was no need to go hungry.

Others had brought offerings to share. Mrs. Springer handed over a jar of peanut butter and a box of Saltines. She'd even remembered a spreader. Leon had brought a couple of tins of deviled ham. Ruth brought tuna fish, and Nancy a sack of apples. They had their dogs, Angus and Millie, in tow. Stella had nuts. George, bologna. Merv's contribution was the best. He'd brought a jug of wine. "And there's plenty more where that came from!" he jovially announced. Laura produced cups, and the party was on.

"Anybody feel like singing?" George timidly asked.

"Great idea!" Ruth chimed in.

And a song fest got underway, with big Merv leading in a strong baritone—

"By the light of the silvery moon
I want to croon
To my honey I'll sing love's tune . . ."

This led into "I'm a Yankee Doodle Dandy . . ."

"When you wore a tulip, a big yellow tulip . . ." and other songs everybody knew, if not the words, at least the melodies to la-de-da along with.

Now and then slight aftershocks of the quake swept through the lobby.

"Here we go again!" roared Merv, prompting him to wave his arms like a band leader, conducting another song.

"Merrily we roll along
Roll along, roll along! . . ."

And the party grew increasingly louder and raucous. Eventually, they ran out of songs. A moody silence pervaded the room, as the candles petered lower.

"Sometimes I wonder why I live in California," Mrs. Springer said.

"Would you rather have hurricanes and tornadoes?" came an answer.

"Wonder when we'll get 'the big one'?" ventured another tenant, referring to frequently published warnings of an earthquake destined to ravish California.

"Not 'til long after we're gone," someone else said.

"I read the year two thousand and ten," said another.

A group groan swept the room.

Laura was desperate to keep everyone's spirits up. "Anybody know a ghost story?" she asked.

"Yes," snapped Helen, who was feeling the effects of the unaccustomed wine. "I'd like to know who killed Elsie Johnson. I bet it was one of us, right here in this room. Maybe *you*, Laura?"

Laura, who was also feeling tipsy, tossed her head in laughter. "Ha-ha-ha! Not me! How about *you*, Mrs. Hudson?" she called out to the hatchet-faced mystery story fan.

"I would never do anything so stupid," Mary Hudson huffily responded.

Timid Mrs. Springer burst into tears.

Mrs. James, leaning over to comfort her, caught Merv staring hollow-eyed at Mary. Really! What an obnoxious man!

Impulsively, she sneered at him, for all to hear, "Why don't you lose some weight, Mr. Allen? You look like an elephant!"

Merv's eyes snapped back to life. And it was suddenly gang-up time on him.

"You *are* too fat," Mrs. Emmons chimed in.

Even Mr. Chin had his say. "Being overweight is not healthy," he added.

"Why, you little twerp!" Merv hollered at him. "You're a fine one to talk. *You'd* look better if you put some *meat* on your bones!"

The four squabbled among themselves.

On the left side of the circle, Stella knelt to pat the mutt, Millie. Leon Levin had been watching for just such an opportunity to speak to her. Sidling behind her, he whispered in her ear, "Why don't you like me?"

Stella turned and looked at him directly. "I never said I didn't," she answered, not her usual strident self at all.

Encouraged by her halfway friendly manner, Leon pulled his chair closer and they sat together, quietly talking.

From across the circle, Mrs. Gannett eyed them fishily, her thin lips tight in disapproval. Although not near enough to hear what they were saying, she was sure they were plotting something evil. A robbery? Maybe another murder! She'd have been astounded to hear their conversation.

"Do you like cats?" Stella had asked Leon, hopefully.

"As a matter of fact, I do!" he told her.

The odd twosome had found a common meeting ground, and were in their own private world, deep in discussion of felines.

Laura was anxious to revitalize the party. She switched on her transistor radio and found a station unique for playing round-the-clock happy music, no matter what calamities might be going on in the outside world.

"Care to dance, George?" Mimi asked. She pulled him to his feet and they bobbed about the center of the circle. Laura joined with Merv, but there not being enough men to go around, the dancing idea soon fizzled. The group, by now numbering about fifty, sat around and listened to the music.

More aftershocks happened, but hysteria had passed. Today's cutting words would be forgotten tomorrow, conquered by the general camaraderie. To the occasional tenant coming home after being caught out in the quake, the lobby scene was most attractive. The flattering light made the ladies look younger, the men more virile. Some of the newcomers stayed to party.

"Hello!" Laura sang out, spotting Bob Delaware, who'd just unlocked the front door and was headed for the stairs. "Come join us!"

"Not tonight!" he waved jovially.

"Well, at least take a flashlight!" she exclaimed, rising and handing one to him.

"You can return it tomorrow."

"OK," he said. "Thanks." He climbed the stairs to the second floor, fanning the darkness before him.

29
Gigi

Inside apartment 210, the poodle, Gigi, had sensed the earthquake coming and had crept, as was her habit upon any upsetting occasion, into the dark calm of Bob Delaware's bedroom closet. As usual, the floor was cluttered with the typical mess of a man living alone. Here a sock, there a sweater fallen off its hanger, a jumble of shoes, a towel, a shirt. Soft things, comforting things to snuggle up among, which she did, head on paws, eyes timorously closed, to wait out the inevitable shake.

Her master had gone out for dinner, but being alone did not upset her. She usually felt relieved when he was not home, so withdrawn had he become lately.

The shaking started, increasing in intensity, sharp vibrations, disturbing sensations. She forced herself to nap through the quake, and when it was over, seeming like an eternity but in reality only seconds later, she stayed in the still of the dark.

Upon the closet shelf, a few things had jostled around, and one of these objects, small, round, and solid, fell and rolled between her paws.

It was not as hard as a nut. Nor did it have the give of a tennis ball. She sniffed it with interest. There was some sort of filling inside that evoked vague instincts of the bird-hunting heritage of her breed. It was an object she had not noticed before, which surprised her for she had carefully checked out the contents of the closet on previous occasions.

There was a sneaker at the back of the closet that had an especially appealing scent. Of blood. A trace was still visible on one of the shoelaces. This newfound thing, too, smelled good; of ripe old leather, and vaguely of meat. She picked it up gently in her mouth to explore. She mouthed it with exquisite care, careful not to bite so as not to damage it.

The feel, the taste, was exceedingly pleasant. She spat it out gently, savouring this new experience, and took it in her mouth again just as the front door opened and Bob entered. His bright torch penetrated the darkness.

"Gigi!" he called. "Where are you? Come, girl!"

Obediently, she sprang to her feet and gaily trotted to the living room. She had the new-found treasure in her mouth, eager to show it to him.

"What have you got there?" He strained to see in the dark. "Come here."

She did, peering up at his thundering tallness.

"Drop it."

She did.

He knelt, and seeing what it was, snatched it quickly, checked its condition, and placed it reverently on a table top. Menacingly, he advanced upon her.

"Don't you ever do that again!" he snarled, slapping her hard on her muzzle.

Stung from the shock of being hit, but more importantly her sensitivities having been assaulted, she slunk, tail down, beneath the dining room table.

He did not speak to her again for the rest of the evening. He sat in the dark, brooding. She remained under the table, trying to be invisible.

30
Cabinet

On the morning after the earthquake, life had returned to normal. No serious damage had been reported in Burlingame. The power was restored. People smiled again. And Win and June, and the big dog Chief, had been drawn like magnets to Elsie's cabinet of trinkets.

The doors had come askew. Nothing had tipped over, not one thing was broken, but June, a neat housekeeper, noticed it immediately—a small round spot toward the back of the topmost shelf. It was bare of the faint veil of dust that had settled around it. "What's missing," she said, pointing, "was right here."

"Funny we didn't notice that on our other searches," Win mused.

"It wasn't there then," she said with conviction. "The quake stirred up the dust, which made the space stand out."

"Bright girl!" he commented.

June felt a tug on the leash, and looked quizzically at Chief. "What's the matter boy? You need to go out?"

The dog signaled with his eyes that he did, but it was not for the reason June thought. Chief had one of his intuitive feelings.

"Be right back, Harry," she said, opening the door. Chief pulled her quickly down the corridor, into the elevator, and outdoors. They reached the sidewalk just as Bob Delaware and Gigi were coming around the corner.

June and Chief had lived together long enough that they picked up on each other's body language. So when Chief's ears snapped to crisp attention and he halted in the path of the advancing pair, June got the message.

"Hello, Mr. Delaware. You seem to be in a hurry."

"I am. I have a tee time. If you'll excuse me . . ."

He started to step around them, but Gigi held back, forcing him to stop short. He glanced down at her, annoyed, and gave her choke-chain a sharp jerk. "Come on girl, I'm late."

Gigi held her ground, puffing out her neck muscles in a way she had learned to counteract the hurting chain.

June, noticing his cruelty, lay a restraining hand on Bob's arm. "You don't have to do that, sir." And, in the next breath, "May I ask you a question?"

"Well, sure," he replied, even more anxious to be on his way, but knowing he'd better seem cooperative.

"I've just come from Mrs. Johnson's apartment. You were a friend of hers, I believe?"

He nodded, evasively.

"Did you ever notice her private collection?" June asked.

"You mean all that junk she kept on display?" he responded, fighting at keeping a calm and uninterested tone to his voice.

"Yes, the little things. Do you remember anything special that she had there?"

"Nope," he shrugged, concentrating hard on seeming casual. "It was just the usual stuff old ladies collect, from what I remember."

"Don't you recall *anything* of particular interest?" she persisted.

"Well, I never looked very closely," he countered. "Didn't know her too well, you know. I wasn't there all that often. Sorry I can't be of more help. Gotta run now, okay?"

"Okay," she smiled, looking him square in the eye. "Thanks." As an afterthought she added, "You sure like your golf, don't you?"

"It's my life," he answered flippantly.

June and Chief stood aside and let them pass. Bob walked rapidly. Gigi trotted beside him, her puffball of a tail held high.

"Hmmmmmm," said June, conversationally to Chief. "Let's go talk to the boss."

They returned to apartment 308, where Win was waiting, comfortably seated on the squashy chintz sofa, a happy grin on his face. An assortment of golf magazines was spread out before him. *Southern Golf, Links, Golf Journal, Fore.*

It crossed June's mind how frivolous he looked reading about golf. At such a time, on duty! She dismissed her fleeting annoyance as he rose to greet them. "So, what was that all about?" he asked.

"Not what you think! We were talking with Mr. Delaware."

"That's interesting," said Win. "I was just thinking about that guy. I'm pretty sure he's our man."

"Well, you'd better hurry if you want to catch him," June replied. "He's on his way to the golf course."

"No kidding?" Win reacted. "That's great!"

He knew that Delaware would be absent for about four hours. It took at least that long to play eighteen holes at hilly Crystal Springs. And if he had a bet going, as he probably did, it would be longer. Plus driving time to and fro. Yes, four hours minimum. Unless he was only going to play nine holes . . . But in that case, they still had a two-hour leeway.

"We need proof," Win said. "Let's go get it."

"Woof!" barked Chief.

For once, this outburst of canine enthusiasm was not shushed by the humans in charge.

Their first step was to get a search warrant, a mission easily accomplished when Win explained to a Burlingame judge his reasons for reasonable suspicion.

Back at the Plaza, Laura, bursting with curiosity, let them into 210. And they began searching Delaware's apartment for something round, small, and very, very valuable.

31
The Treasure

Where to begin?

The poodle, Gigi, eager to help, welcomed the trio with a wide-mouthed grin. She bowed submissively before the large, handsome shepherd.

"What are we looking for, Harry?" June asked.

"A motive for murder," he said.

As if understanding the words, Gigi whined to catch their attention. Succeeding, she rolled her eyes toward Bob Delaware's bedroom/office, indicating that they should go there. She led the way, loping the few steps gaily.

Quickly, the team moved to the desk and opened drawers, rummaging the contents with experienced hands.

"Nothing in this one," June reported, sifting through a mishmash of notepads, lip balm, eyeglass cleaner, pens, and Kleenex.

"Nor here," Win replied, rifling through writing paper, stapler, stamps, paper clips, and a small flask of whiskey.

They moved to the computer and printer. Nothing suspicious there.

They looked behind and beneath his typewriter. Nothing.

They searched a cart on wheels. It was chockablock with the ordinary tools of a writer's trade. Nothing more.

They moved on to Delaware's bookcase. It had three shelves, and Win eyed enviously the writer's collection of golf books—so much more complete than his own.

"There must be at least a hundred books here," he said to June, awed.

Giving a short appreciative whistle, he gazed swiftly from top shelf to bottom. There was everything from Harvey Penick's *Little Red Book* to Robert Clark's *Golf: A Royal and Ancient Game.*

Win found himself staring compellingly at the middle shelf. His eyes were drawn to a heavy, hollow glass brick that was serving as a bookend. "There it is!" he said, triumphantly.

"What is?" June demanded to know.

Gigi, looking on, barked with excitement. How she'd love to mouth the thing again!

Carefully, Win reached into the glass brick, a handkerchief wrapped around his hand so as not to destroy Delaware's fingerprints. He removed the tiny treasure that had been stashed inside. Gently cradling it in the palm of his hand, he showed it to June.

"What is it?" she asked, mystified.

"It's a featherie," he explained. "One of the world's first-known golf balls."

"For heaven's sake," she said, scoffing, "why do you call it 'feathery'? Looks like a balled-up wad of leather to me."

"That's just what it is," he explained patiently, holding it as gingerly as Gigi had done.

"It's a leather bag. But it's stuffed with feathers on the inside. See that stitching? It holds together a top-hatful of feathers. Incredible, yes?"

She had to admit it was.

He continued. "For over three hundred years, 'goffers,'

as they were called then, played with this kind of ball.

"For maybe three hundred years before the 'featherie,' balls were made of wood."

"But wooden balls would hurt if they struck other players, right?" June commented lightly, recalling her one time on a golf course when she had shanked a shot that narrowly missed hitting a golfer on a parallel fairway.

Wrapped in emotion, Harry only half heard her flip remark and went on with his soliloquy.

"Featheries were last used about 1890, if I'm recalling my golf history right. Do you remember seeing that *Architects of Golf* book at my place?"

June smiled condescendingly.

"It tells all that sort of thing. So," he continued in a respectful tone of voice, "this little baby is at least a century old.

"I've read there are only about three hundred featheries left in the world, all in private collections. Oh, look!" he said, turning it carefully. "It's even been signed by the craftsman who made it! This is worth a fortune!"

In his enthusiasm, he was giving her far more of an explanation than she thought necessary. Hands on hips, she shifted her weight from one leg to the other and gave a small bored sort of sigh. Still rapt in reverie, Win ignored her.

"This little ball," he continued, "could fly like a devil if a golfer hit it correctly. It was also likely to burst on impact. On a rainy day, it could just disintegrate. One way or another, a golfer could break a lot of these during a game. Even a hundred years ago, golf balls were expensive. Why, they could cost as much as a golf club!

"The featherie is why they had to invent a more practical type of golf ball. So that people could afford to play. They made balls of gutta-percha after this."

"Gotta what?!" June laughed derisively. Really! Win's lecture was getting out of control.

"Gut-ta-per-cha," he said again, slowly and distinctly. "It's the same stuff dentists use today for making fillings."

She looked at him incredulously, torn between laughing and being serious.

He wasn't through yet.

"Of course, these days golf balls are made of synthetics. Balata and surlyn, that sort of stuff. God, isn't this beautiful?" he exclaimed again. "I never thought I'd see a featherie outside of a museum!" Tenderly, he fondled it, handkerchief firmly in place, while Gigi drooled and even Chief showed a flicker of interest.

"So," he told June, coming out of his reverie, "This is our motive. This ancient little ball. Obviously, it was taken from the victim's collection."

"It *is* the right size," June agreed, seeing in her mind's eye the small round vacant place in Elsie Johnson's cabinet.

"Yes, I believe a devout golfer could kill for this," Win mused. "It's so rare, it's history. It's also extremely valuable. Worth thousands to a private collector. Ten thousand dollars, easily. Maybe even twenty."

"For that ugly little thing?" June responded. *Honestly,* she thought, *Harry can be so fuddy-duddy. I wish he'd get to the point.*

Now it was Win's turn to sigh. "Someday," he said, "you'll get interested in golf. And when you do, you'll realize that any link to its past is priceless. And this *isn't* ugly!" he added, defensively. "It's beautiful!"

"If you say so," she grudgingly nodded. "But how," she asked, eager to get him back on track, "are we going to prove that Elsie owned it, and that Delaware took it, and probably killed her for it?"

"Elementary, my dear," he said, loftily.

"All we need to do is to find that one more thing that will clinch it."

The poodle barked, and trotted to the closet where she'd lain during the earthquake. She was eager to show them her other soft find. So absorbed were Win and June in the drama of the moment that each flinched in surprise at the angry voice behind them.

"What the hell are you doing here?"

Bob Delaware had come home from golf, earlier than expected.

32
Why?

Seeing the precious featherie in the detective's hand, Delaware took a belligerent step forward, as if to wrest it from him. Suddenly he froze. An aghast expression crossed his face. For his dog, Gigi, was emerging from the closet, her jaws clamped around the other plaything.

It was one of the sneakers he'd worn the night of Elsie's death. Its lace dangled tauntingly and Win's face lit with heightened interest, noticing its telltale feature.

Kneeling to accept the shoe from the dog, he patted her gratefully. She preened with pleasure. "Thanks, girl," he said.

"Oh, God," muttered Bob.

Win was examining with excruciating attention the small brownish stain on the lacing. It was a trace of dried blood. Elsie Johnson's, Win was sure. He was so sure that the crime lab would confirm it that he declared, "Mr. Delaware, I am arresting you on suspicion of murder. You have the right to remain silent . . ."

"Oh, shut up," Bob interrupted with an exasperated wave of his hand. "I'll tell you what happened."

June and Win stood facing him, ready to listen. The dogs sat watching, side by side.

Delaware sighed deeply—a sigh of both regret and relief. The game was over.

"She'd invited me in for a drink," Bob began. "It wasn't the first time. I'd been there before. Nothing romantic. After all, she's—" he caught himself— "*was*—old enough to be my mother. About as annoying, too," he added wryly.

"And?" Win prompted.

"I'd noticed the featherie before," said Delaware. "She never let guests in the kitchen when she was mixing drinks. I guess you've heard that?"

They nodded.

"So while I was waiting for my drink, I'd walk around her room and look at things. I couldn't believe it when I first saw the featherie." He smiled wistfully at the memory. "There it was, just plunked behind the glass doors, crammed in with all that other stuff she had! Geez, she didn't even know what it was. I had to explain it to her.

" 'Oh, is that so?' she'd said." (He mimicked her coquettish voice.) "That just about drove me crazy. The old fool. She had no idea of its wonderful history. St. Andrews . . . Carnoustie . . . Old Tom Morris . . ." His eyes glazed over, like a curtain falling, but then shot open again.

"She didn't give a hoot about golf. She only kept it because someone had told her it was worth a lot. She wasn't even curious enough to know why." He shook his head in scornful disbelief.

Win and June remained silent. Catching the importance of the occasion, the dogs, too, stayed still, although their eyes darted between each member of the trio.

"Well," Bob continued with his confession, "I kept thinking about the featherie. It was always in the back of my mind. I even dreamt about it. Every time I went down there it killed me to see it just—" he gestured helplessly— "there.

"This last time, for some reason she'd left the key in the cabinet. I'd had a couple of belts before going to see her, so I was feeling pretty relaxed. While she was out of the room, I went to it and, well, naturally, I unlocked it and reached in and got the featherie. I closed the cabinet quietly. I didn't think she'd notice.

"Gad, what a gorgeous thing! It was such a thrill to hold it; even if just for a moment. It was like touching history, you know?"

Win nodded. In his golfer's heart, he knew something of the passion Delaware sought to explain.

"So," Bob sighed, recalling the fateful evening, "she came out of the kitchen, carrying our drinks, and well, you'd have thought I'd stolen the crown jewels.

" 'Put that back,' she yelled. Actually, screeched is more like it.

"Well, I was really surprised at her reaction. I thought it was a pretty innocent thing I'd done. I mean, what golfer wouldn't want to touch an honest-to-god featherie? I tried to jolly her along.

" 'Oh, come on,' I remember saying, 'You don't care about this thing. I'd appreciate it much more than you. How about letting me have it?'

" 'No!' she said.

" 'Let me *buy* it then! How much would you sell it to me for?'

"The damn woman. 'That's out of the question!' she hollered. 'Put it back this instant!' " (In a falsetto voice, he mimicked her again.)

"Okay, so what I did was stupid. I teased her. I put it in my pocket. I honestly thought she was kidding, being uppity just to be dramatic. I thought after a drink or two she'd give in and let me have it.

"Some drink!" He spat out the words. "I never did get it. She put my glass down and came at me in such an arrogant way I literally saw red. She started to grab the featherie. God! What a dumb broad! It could have burst open!

"I knew, then, I had to have it. That damn fool would ruin it, and then *nobody* could enjoy it. So I grabbed her around the neck. I didn't mean to choke her. I was just trying to shake some sense into her, you know? I mean, she was like a crazy woman."

June bit her lip, stifling an impulse to slap him.

Bob went on. "I suddenly realized what I was doing. Hell, I'd just about strangled her. Her eyes were bulging. She was gasping. I let go fast. She stumbled backwards. She lost her balance and fell against that damn, heavy chair with all the carvings on top. It belonged in some museum, not in a little apartment, for God's sake. It was like slow motion, you know?"

His onlookers nodded.

"She hit the side of her head. Real hard. I could hear the crack. She just kept falling. I knelt to see if there was some way I could help her. There wasn't much blood. I thought maybe she'd just passed out. But she wasn't breathing. And she was so still. Her eyes, so glassy." A shocked expression crossed his face.

"I knew then that she was dead. But it's not as if I meant to kill her. It was an accident, see?" He looked at them pleadingly.

Solemnly, Win shook his head.

"I panicked," admitted Delaware. "So I got out of there. Fast."

"And with the featherie," Win added, a tinge of sarcasm in his voice.

"Yuh, well, she didn't need it anymore," Delaware rebutted.

"What did you do then?" pressed June, struggling to keep her emotions in check.

"I went home. I took the backstairs. Nobody saw me."

"Thank you, sir," Win said to Delaware. "You've been very cooperative. But you'll have to come with us to the station now."

"Before we leave, tell me one thing, will you?" Bob asked.

"Sure," said Win.

"What led you to me?"

"It was what you *didn't* tell us," Win answered, matter-of-factly.

Bob looked puzzled. Win explained.

"Do you remember when Officer Jacobs first called on you, when we were making our rounds of the tenants?"

"Yuh."

"You said you hardly knew Mrs. Johnson. But on her coffee table was a golf magazine. It had an article that had been marked to be noticed. It was written by one Bob Woods."

"So?" said Bob Delaware, pretending to be perplexed.

"We found other golf magazines, dated other months, around her apartment. All had articles in them by this Mr. Woods. It took us awhile to make the connection, but that's your pen name, right?"

Delaware shrugged, jutting out his chin with a nervous hitch.

Win continued.

"The mailing labels were still on the magazines, so we knew Mrs. Johnson didn't buy them. And they were all addressed to the subscriber. To Bob Woods. To *you*."

Bob shrugged again. "So?"

"So," Win went on, patiently, "some of these magazines are more than a year old. I'm glad you're doing well as a writer, Mr. Delaware, but you weren't very smart to brag about it. You left quite a trail at Mrs. Johnson's. You've known her for a long time."

Bob slapped his forehead. "Stupid jerk!" he muttered at himself.

"If you'll come with us now," Win interceded.

"I can't!" Bob yelled, wild-eyed. "I've got a deadline!"

Impulsively, he made a break for the door. He was too slow. With a bound, Chief was there before him, hackles rising, blocking the way, and snarling.

"Freeze!" June ordered Delaware.

He obeyed.

Chief backed off but remained on alert.

"You'd better cuff Mr. Delaware," Win advised her.

Firmly holding Bob's wrists, she did.

She and Win stood aside so that Delaware, herded by Chief, would precede them out. Partway through the doorway, he turned and glanced at his dog. Gigi had assumed the "Sit –Stay" position. Her lustrous brown eyes were somber and serious. "Man's best friend. Ha!" he snorted, wheeling on his heel and leaving.

Last one out of the door of apartment 210 was June. She smiled reassuringly at the poodle. "We'll be back to get you, girl," she said.

33
Loose Ends

Confession taken. And on what remained of Thursday and Friday, the case was wrapped up.

Delaware's fingerprints had proved a match for the prints Win's men had pulled from Elsie's doorknob, cabinet, and the back of the chair Bob had grasped momentarily while leaning toward her body to check her condition. Delaware had also left his distinctive prints around her neck, and, of course, on the tiny featherie. The infinitesimal bit of her blood on his shoelace was conclusive. Delaware was there. He had killed her.

It was now Saturday morning, and June and Win were rewarding themselves with a run on the Sawyer Camp Trail. How delectable she looked in her flared pink trunks, he thought. To her, he looked sexy too in his clingy whites.

The day was particularly dramatic. Puffy clouds scudded across the sky. Whitecaps sparkled on the water.

At the five-mile-marker there was a bench, and they stopped to admire the view.

"Can we sit for a while and talk?" she asked.

"Of course."

"What's bothering you?" he asked intuitively, taking her hand.

"Well, for starters, Harry, how can it be called murder when Delaware didn't actually kill her? It really was an accident, wasn't it?"

"Not in the eyes of the law," Win explained. "It was murder because he provoked it. She would not have died that night if he hadn't caused it to happen. Of course, there are many degrees of murder. It's up to the district attorney which one Delaware gets charged with. My guess is it will be negligent manslaughter."

"Why wasn't there more blood at the death scene?" she wondered. "I thought head wounds bled a lot."

"Because of the nature of the blow, she bled inside her brain," he answered bluntly. "She sustained a massive hemorrhage. She truly died instantaneously from blood flooding her head."

"Oh," June reacted, blanching.

"Got another question?" he asked, more softly.

"Yes," she said. "It took us ten days to solve this case. Is that about normal?"

"Some go quicker. Some drag on. Some never get solved," he answered. "Of course," he added, with a grin, "I had exceptional help on this case. The dogs and you. That saved a lot of time."

A faint smile escaped her lips, but she was still in a serious frame of mind. "What will happen to Delaware now?" she asked.

"Well, there's no bail for murder so he's in custody until the judicial process takes over. What kind of sentence he'll get will depend on how skillful his lawyer is and, if it goes to trial, on the jury."

"What about his dog?" June asked. "Since Delaware is going to be so busy with court appearances, who'll look after her?"

"Leave it to you to think of that!" Win said, fondly. "She could be farmed out to a kennel, I suppose."

"Over my dead body!" June exclaimed.

"Let's not have any more of those!" he laughed.

"*I* can take her in," she said. "I'm sure Chief wouldn't mind. The dogs seem to like each other."

"That would be a very generous offer to make Delaware," Win commented.

"Yeah, well, I don't think he's overly fond of the dog anyway," she said.

"It's obvious to me he doesn't care about *anybody*," Win declared. "The man has no scruples. So what else is worrying you?"

"Well, Harry, if you didn't happen to be a golfer yourself, how on earth would you have known what a featherie was, and figured out how it tied in with Mrs. Johnson's death?"

"You see? Golf isn't a waste of time after all!" he answered her lightly.

Again, her face reflected that liberated woman's look he found so endearing, especially when he compared it with the vulnerable side of her that he felt he now knew so well. She deserved more of an answer than his flip one, so he told her something of the all-absorbing interest he felt in being an investigator—of the necessity to have a smattering of education on many subjects—to be always learning. "You never know what odd bit of knowledge will come in handy. Nothing in life is wasted in police work. Enough of lecture!" he laughed. "Got another?"

"Yes, Harry. The damn featherie itself. What happens to *it* now?"

"I suppose you think *I* have it?" he smiled.

"You *don't?!*" she reacted, shocked.

"No, of course not," he assured her. "It's sealed in a plastic pouch, locked up safe in a police vault, until it's needed for evidence. And there's plenty of that. Delaware's prints are all over it, as well as some saliva smears, thanks to his four-footed friend."

"What happens to the featherie afterwards?" she persisted.

"It's in the laps of the gods," he told her.

"Oh, come on," she urged, assuming he was keeping inside information from her.

"No, it really *is*," he explained. "Mrs. Johnson did not leave a will. She probably meant to, but never got around to it. Maybe she considered herself invincible. She hadn't been to a doctor for years, either. The only service people she saw regularly were her stockbroker and her hairdresser. Anyway, what's ironic is that the featherie is considered part of her estate, and it would go to her heirs. But she didn't name any. So it will be up to the judge to decide who gets it."

"All that wealth, all those nice possessions, and not even *charity* gets it?" June exclaimed.

"Well," Win went on, "I guess you could call the state of California a charity. It's practically broke, you know. That's probably who'll get it all by default. And then the featherie would be auctioned for cash. Imagine that! I might have a chance of owning it, after all!" (*Fat chance on my salary,* he thought, wryly).

"So," he added, "what else is on your pretty little mind?"

"The *people,* Harry. What about all the people who we thought, early on, might be guilty?"

"They were a colorful bunch, weren't they!" he chuckled. "Well, let's see . . .

"Mr. Levin and Miss Rankin seem on the way to becoming a duo. Mr. Allen, now . . . if he can get that temper of his under control, he just might be able to get that bread business going. Maybe he'll sign up the Bit of England for starters. As for Mimi, well, I don't know what to say about her . . ."

"You'd better not!" June laughed.

"Maybe Mr. Schmidt will make an honest woman of

her!" Win said, with a wink.

"Do you think anyone besides George had a key to Mrs. Johnson's?" June asked him.

"I doubt it," Win opined. "From what we learned about the victim, she didn't trust many people. Certainly not Levin or Mr. Allen. Or even Bob Delaware."

"You know," June said wistfully, "I'm going to miss the Dog House."

"We could stop by now and then to say hello," he told her. "I, too, feel we've made some friends there. On the whole, it was a happy experience."

"Except for Elsie Johnson," June reminded him.

"Oh, I've been meaning to tell you!" he exclaimed.

"There was something else interesting in her autopsy report. It showed that her arteries were very calcified. In other words, she was well on the way to developing hardening of the arteries. She'd have been a prime candidate soon for a coronary or a heart attack. Mr. Delaware may have done her a favor."

June, who had been gazing into space, looked at him, surprised. "And what else have you forgotten to tell me, Harry?"

She couldn't have given him a better cue. "I love you, June."

She smiled, demurely at first, and then with a wide look of pleasure. *Harry may have some fussy ways,* she thought, *but he is very sweet, and dear. And he had sex appeal, too.* She doubted she could do any better. She decided on the spot to commit herself.

"You gorgeous man!" she said. "I love you, too!"

He tilted her chin toward his, and they kissed, sweetly, deeply, tenderly.

Runners passing by looked over at them. And grinned, and applauded.

34
Epilogue

It was the start of a new month, and Laura Fiedler, manager of the Park Plaza, had risen early to do dusting and polishing and to set up on the sidewalk the red and white "Vacancy" sign. She had no sooner turned to her ledger to begin entering the rent payments than the manager's bell sounded from outside the building.

She peered through the glass window. The person looked presentable. *Very* nice, in fact. She was a senior citizen, tall, stately, silver-haired, well-dressed, and she had a King Charles Spaniel on a leash.

Yes, quite acceptable, Laura thought.

She bustled to the entrance, and opened the door, beaming.

"Do you allow pets?" the queenly woman asked.

"We do," acknowledged Laura. "If it is well-behaved."

"Mine most certainly is," the woman sniffed. "And you have an apartment available?" she demanded to know.

"As a matter of fact," replied Laura, "we have two."